DATE DUE			
JAN 8	MAY 1 04 04		
JAN 26 01	AUG 10 04 04		
FEB 14 01			
MAR 20 '01			
APR 13 '01			
MAY 7 01			
JUN 6 01			
SEP 28 01			
OCT 12 01			
OCT 26 01			
JAN 14 02			
MAR 28 03			

12/00

JACKSON COUNTY
Library Services

HEADQUARTERS
413 West Main Street
Medford, Oregon 97501

Open Land

Open Land

B. M. BOWER

Sagebrush
Large Print Westerns

Library of Congress Cataloging-in-Publication Data

Bower, B.M., 1874-1940
  Open land / B.M. Bower.
    p.   cm.
  ISBN 1-57490-288-1 (alk. paper)
  1. Large type books. I. Title

  PS3503.O8193 O64 2000
  813'.52—dc21   00-040275

Cataloguing in Publication Data is available from
the British Library and the National Library of Australia.

Sagebrush Large Print Westerns are published in the United
States and Canada by Thomas T. Beeler, Publisher, PO Box 659,
Hampton Falls, New Hampshire 03844-0659. ISBN 1-57490-288-1

Published in the United Kingdom, Eire, and the Republic of
South Africa by Isis Publishing Ltd, 7 Centremead, Osney
Mead, Oxford OX2 0ES England. ISBN 0-7531-6261-X

Published in Australia and New Zealand by Bolinda Publishing
Pty Ltd, 17 Mohr Street, Tullamarine, 3043, Victoria, Australia.
ISBN 1-74030-017-3

Manufactured by Sheridan Books in Chelsea, Michigan.

Open Land

CHAPTER ONE

TEN MILES OUT ON THE FORT BENTON ROAD, THAN pulled up and dismounted in a sheltered hollow where the sulphur fumes, belching day and night from the great smelter stack, had not blasted shrub and soil. From the coarse and blackened crust of an old snowbank clear water seeped and trickled down a rock ledge with a faint tinkling sound where it dropped to the gravel wash below. A little pool was there, and on the low bank just beyond, a few tufts of sand grass were showing green next the roots. Farther along the wash grew other tufts of green. While he stood there looking, mildly surprised at a vague tightening in his chest, a meadowlark swooped unafraid down to a wild sunflower stalk that had withstood the buffetings of winter storms. There it swayed and sang its brief exultant melody, then hopped to the ground and drank from the tiny rill where it spilled over the ledge in a miniature waterfall.

While his horse nosed and nibbled amongst the dwarfed wild currant bushes, Than eased himself down upon a warm boulder and stared hard at the bird. The first meadowlark. March was yet in its first week, but spring was here, sure enough. Meadowlarks knew.

The bird drank its fill of sun-melted snow, preened itself for a moment or two, thought of something urgent and flew off over the low ridge. Than drew a deep slow breath and mounted his rangy black. Moody, an undefined ache in his breast, he rode slowly back up the ridge, following the bird.

Now the huge smokestack towered into the smiling blue, flecked with lazy white clouds. Endlessly spewed

1

from the blackened hill beneath it, an enormous python of smoke writhed away toward the Highwoods. Greenish yellow where it emerged heavy with the blighting fumes of sulphur, darker where the light breeze fanned the coal smoke upward to higher currents, the smelter stack and its endless reeling smoke wreath dominated the near landscape.

Again Than sighed, lips pressed together. His eyes ranged farther. Cutting the town, second only to the smokestack in importance, flowed the broad sliding ribbon of silver that was the Missouri; beyond the town a narrower, bluer band that was Sun River; beyond that still, Sun River Bench, brown and flat, with steep wrinkled edges like a gigantic pie dropped bottom up between the two rivers; towering above it still farther away, the abrupt four-cornered eminence they called Square Butte. Thirty, forty miles off it stood—and looked an hour's ride from the brown trail where he jogged boredly along at a leisurely pace. Away in the distance, beyond Square Butte, a pale violet-and-silver etching against the horizon, stood the Rockies, looking as remote, as serenely unattainable, as the thin crescent of moon standing ethereal above their highest peak.

Distance. The winds of heaven blowing across untracked prairies; the low of cattle filing down from the upland ranges to loiter knee-deep in some willow-fringed pool; smell of rain sweeping across the grassy slopes at dusk, muted drumming of the first great drops on stretched canvas; splitting crash of lightning-rent storm clouds; old songs endlessly intoned while one sleepily circled a slumbering herd, bedded at dusk on some grassy knoll. These things called from the soft violet distances. Listening to the first lark song, a hunger for the open range awoke to a poignant craving.

No longer vague, that aching heaviness within his breast; in two words he could define it! Round-up time.

Of course it wasn't actually round-up time. It wouldn't be for two months yet. But it was coming, just as surely as the first fuzzy-stemmed crocuses, making each grassy slope a carpet of blue. He counted the weeks mentally. Three of March, four in April—May— If this weather held, the wagons ought to be rolling by the first of May. The tenth, anyway. Maybe by that time he'd be able to persuade his mother that Dade was old enough to take care of himself and didn't need a dry nurse.

He'd round Dade up and talk to him like a Dutch uncle—make him cut out that bunch of town smarties he was running with. Money—Dade seemed to think whisky and cards and fast women couldn't pull a man down, so long as he sought them in a rich man's parlor— —that coughing up blood—that was just whisky and cigarettes and rolling 'em high, night after night. He'd have to put a stop to Dade's carousing before his mother found out.

The black's little fox trot ate up the miles. Than was still dreaming of the open ranges when he rode down through the scattered shacks and plain smoke-grimed little houses that formed the vanguard of North Great Falls' sporadic growth. The town itself lay across the river. Directly below him, Black Eagle Falls surged thunderously down upon the walled river bank where the monstrous smelters crouched upon the bluff's precipitous side. An ore train heavily laden with rich copper ore from Anaconda came snaking down along the river's bank, and the fireman, who knew Than by sight, pulled the whistle cord violently as train and horseman reached the trestle together. The black

3

snorted, reared and pivoted while the fireman leaned from his window and chortled at the show as the train passed under the bridge. Than brought the horse around and went tearing out of sight behind the railing. So the fireman drew in his head and settled to his duty, his face still wearing a boyish grin not unmixed with envy.

A hatred of the sprawling overgrown town seized Than. He rode recklessly, superbly, scattering chickens and a yelping dog or two as he went. A sober-minded motorman munching a sandwich while he sent his little empty street car bucking along the uneven rails wound the brake handle frantically and let a crumb go down his windpipe when Than rode headlong across the track directly in front of him. Than never gave him a glance.

These things the north side of town had learned to endure. When he reached the neat tree-bordered street where the Roberts house stood primly behind its white picket fence, Than pulled the black down to his gentle fox trot. He was glad of his sedate pace when he saw his mother just turning in at the gate. His inner monitor warned him that something was amiss. Dade, probably. His elder-brother sense of responsibility nudged him uncomfortably with the thought that he should have made it his business to know just where Dade had been last night and why he had not come home until dawn was streaking the east. But damn it, Dade was twenty-two. Old enough to have some sense.

His mother stood holding the gate with two tightly gloved hands, watching his approach. For once she was not smiling. "Come in, Jonathan, as soon as you've put up your horse. I want to talk to you."

"Spade can stand for a while. What's wrong? Dade?" He had not meant to jump at that conclusion, but the word slipped out.

4

"I've been to the doctor with David. That cough of his—I don't like the way it's been hanging on. The boy's working too hard—"

Than winced. Probably she had not meant to reproach him, but a month's idleness had made him sensitive. "He's running around too much nights," he said bluntly.

His mother's glance sharpened. "Jonathan, be fair, if you can't be friendly. You know as well as I do—"

"Good glory, Mom! Haven't I always been more than fair and friendly to Dade? To hear you talk—"

"Now, don't fly off the handle, Thannie. I was just quotin' a saying my father always used. You go right on and take care of Black Hawk, and then come into the settin' room. We've got to do something about Dade and we might as well make up our minds to do it cheerful. I've got a plan I want to talk over. Go right along and stop your scowling. You look blacker than Hawk does."

Jonathan grinned ruefully and did as he was told. With a mother like that, even an upstanding young man of twenty-five cannot easily forget the habit of obedience. He was still resolutely smiling when he hung his gray range hat on its accustomed ivory-tipped peg just above the diamond-shaped plate-glass mirror in the old walnut hall tree and went into the sitting room where his mother and his nineteen-year-old sister Susan awaited him.

The room wore an atmosphere of solemnity. Even Sue's face was sobered. The dreams of the morning fled from Than, leaving him older, with grave steadfast eyes and shoulders squared to carry the burden of responsibility for these two and the wild headstrong brother who must not bring a heartache to the womenfolk.

5

He closed the door behind him, closing also a mental door that had opened upon hard-riding cowboys galloping across the springy sod where flowers nodded in the new grass, and upon canvas-covered wagons lurching across the rangeland toward some hidden spring or a full-running stream. That door must not open again, he thought swiftly, as he made his way across the furniture-cluttered room and sat down with his back to the window where a soft spring breeze tugged maddeningly at the lace curtains. It must not pull him to the round-up. His place was here, looking after the family.

CHAPTER TWO

IN THE LAND OFFICE NEXT DAY THAN LEANED BOTH elbows and half his body upon the wide desk, poring over a map. It was astonishing to discover how much territory came under the jurisdiction of the Great Falls land office. Than had thought he knew the country pretty well, but he felt lost and more than a little confused before this bald expense of townships, section squares and range-this-and-that. Dickey Blake, assiduously chewing mint gum while he lounged within the railed-off space, could not help him. Than was thinking impatiently that Dickey might be a wizard behind that desk but he probably thought these darned map lines were drawn with a rule upon valley and hill. It would be a lot simpler if they were, he reflected.

At that precise moment some one slapped him on the back so enthusiastically that Than's nose was pushed against the map. A voice quite as hearty greeted him.

"Hello Than, you old highbinder! Glad to see you!

What the blue blazes have you got your nose glued to that plat for?"

"Cause you stuck it there. Good glory! If you were any gladder you'd use a sledge hammer, I s'pose." Than wrinkled his nose tentatively, then rubbed his fingers across his upper lip and examined them for blood.

"Sorry," the newcomer apologized.

Dickey gave an abrupt chortle and expertly shifted his gum to the other side of his mouth. "Yes, he's sorry!" he jibed. "What Blaney needs is to be laid out cold some day. He don't knock my backbone into my teeth like that, yuh notice."

Dickey was a flat-chested little fellow with a permanent stoop. Blaney looked him over. "Maybe I would if I could find it—and was glad enough to see you," he retorted, with the heavy-handed freedom of a perfect friendship.

Than facetiously drew back his fist. "How are you?— Before I swat you down."

"Fine and dandy, and I can lick you any time, any place, any old way, with one hand tied behind me."

"Gosh, you're feeling foxy." Than dropped an open palm to the desk. "Didn't even know you were back."

"Just got in this morning." Blaney was a special agent for the district land office and his duties carried him far afield. He lifted himself to the counter and sat swinging his long legs while he talked of his trip.

Times were changed, he deplored. Fences stood where fences never were thought of five years ago, when he and Than had fared joyously forth to be cowboys, one bed roll shared between them; one air castle as well, which they gravely builded together on many a long and lonely ride. Cattle kings they would be, nothing less. Five years they had given themselves to

7

gather the nucleus of their vast herds. Ten years should see them independent. Well, five years saw neither owning a hoof of his first cow. Blaney had somehow drifted into his present job. Than still called himself a puncher, but with months in town holding the Roberts family together since his father died, the term was almost a figure of speech.

Neither spoke of these things today. For a while they gossiped of men and places and trivial happenings, then Than lifted his arm off the map of Northern Montana and stared down with vague discouragement in his eyes.

Blaney, feeling for a match to light the cigarette he had just rolled, eyed him sidelong. "What's eating you, Than? Want to be a gentle farmer and hoe spuds?" His tone was quizzical, his eyes warm with a deep friendliness.

"Something like that." Than looked up with the grin he had carried into his mother's sitting room yesterday. "Maybe not spuds—I hope not. But on the dead, I'm looking for land. The Roberts family is willing to accept a hunk from our Uncle Sammy. The burning question right now is, what hunk?"

Blaney's eyes left Than's face and dropped for a cursory glance at the plat, a glance which betrayed a bored familiarity with its thousand details. He looked again at Than.

"Better not tackle it," he advised. "Looks like a snap, on paper. On the ground, it's a dog's life—unless you've got capital. Even with money to go ahead on, it's no picnic, believe me."

Than straightened. "I know all that, Blaney, and a lot you forgot to mention. It's a case of got to, in a way. Far as the money goes, we'll have that, all right. Mother's got a buyer for our place. Six thousand cash. She's been

8

holding off, not wanting to sell, but now she's made up her mind to do it. We've got a little besides that. We'll squeak along, all right."

Blaney continued to look at Than studyingly. He shook his head, unconvinced. "I thought you were going to work for the T L this spring," he observed with seeming irrelevance.

"So did I, if—" Than closed his mouth, glanced from Blaney to Dick and back again. "I'll tell you boys, and ask you to keep it under your hats, both of you. Mother's worried to death over Dade."

"Say, you can't tell me anything about Dade I don't know," Dickey cut in wisely. "I was out with him to a party, a week or so ago. Wow!"

"Yeah," Than laconically agreed. "Wow and more wow. A few more months here in town and it'll be the bow-wows. He's got a cough that's hung on since last fall and it's getting worse. Mom dragged him off to a doctor yesterday and the verdict is, he's to get outa town and stay out. So—"

"Why don't you take him on round-up?" Blaney suggested.

Than shook his head. "He'd last quick with the T L, and you know it. Time old Wooden Shoes watched him stand on his head a few times, Dade would be given his time. He can't rope and he can't ride. About all he can do is push a pencil days and raise hell nights." He flung out an expressive hand, laughing constrainedly. "Not that I'm a tin saint myself or want to knock baby brother. But it's my job to look after him and keep him straight, and he's getting out of hand here in town."

"David and Jonathan," Blaney said under his breath, an odd look in his eyes.

"Well, not exactly. But Mom seems to expect

9

something of the sort. Anyway, taking care of the family is my job and I can't do it here. Mom wants to use our homestead rights, and I'd just as soon ranch for a living as plug around town, working for some other fellow. I hate the damn place. So now you know. Come across, old-timer," he laughed gamely. "Put me wise to a good location. That's your job, darn yuh. I'll get that kid into the hills and straighten him out or wring his blamed neck."

Through three slow pulls of his cigarette Blaney meditated upon the matter. "What sort of ranch do you want?" he finally asked, scraping off his cigarette ash against the desk edge. "Stock or spuds? Dry land or irrigated? Hay land, grain land, grazing—got any idea at all, or are you just going it blind?"

"Well—not so blamed blind as you sound. Edge of the hills somewhere, maybe, where there's water, shelter and woods, opening out on a creek bottom; something like that. Better not be too close to any town. Don't want it too easy for Dade to beat it in there. Twenty or thirty miles—a good day's drive, say. I'd like to raise a few head of cattle and some horses, and cut hay enough to feed them, and maybe raise a little grain for chickens and pigs."

He straightened, pushed back his gray hat and laughed with some embarrassment. "Good glory! You ought to know as much about it as I do, Blaney. Just a nice, homey, all-purpose ranch where we can make a decent living and the women can raise flowers and chickens and be comfortable. Mom'll want to milk cows and have lots of butter and cream and eggs to cook with. She said so. And Sue's plumb batty over horseback riding. You know." Again that outflung gesture with one hand, which could express so much.

10

"Hm-mm." Blaney twisted his body around so that he could fling his cigarette stub into the big nickel cuspidor. "Just a choice hunk of the moon with a fence around it. That's the idea, hunh?"

"No, a ranch like that ought to be possible with a few years of buckling right down to hard work."

"Well, maybe—emphasizing the hard work. What rights have you got, Than?"

"Quite a few. Mother's got Dad's soldier right, three years knocked off for service. And I've got my homestead right and so has Dade. Sue's too young. I was looking for a chunk big enough so all our claims could join." He grinned. "Kinda want to go the whole hog, I guess."

Dickey Blake was leaning forward from his side of the desk. "That oughta be easy," he remarked. "There's plenty of open land left." He glanced down at the map.

Blaney also looked down at it. "Most of it isn't worth a damn, though," he stated disparagingly. "Prairie-dog towns or rocks or 'dobe. Open land enough—I should say yes! Just as it lays on the map. When you ride out over it, though, you begin to see the good land's been snapped up. The sort of place Than wants—" He fell silent, absently scanning township after township, county after county, while he searched his memory for the ideal location for the ranch Than had pictured.

"Say," he said abruptly, "I know the place—the *exact* place you want. But—" He hunched his shoulders, frowning down at a certain spot among the numbered squares. His whole body relaxed, as if he were physically letting go the idea.

"But what? Ain't it open?" Than's eyes were suddenly eager. "What's the joker—or isn't there any?"

Blaney gave a short laugh. "You bet your sweet life

11

there's a joker. She's a peach of a place, all right. A full section up in the Broken Hills country. Plenty of good water—a trout creek runs through the middle of it. Fine soil, some pine timber and all kinds of quakin' asp and alder, with a cottonwood grove on the creek; Running Man Creek, they call it up there. Plenty of pasture land––"

"Sounds made to order." Than could not quite keep the jubilance out of his voice. "What's wrong with it, Blaney?"

"Nothing. Not a thing in the world. Only," drawled Blaney, "a big cow outfit has got it covered; fenced in with a big field of theirs. It's government land, all right, open to settlement. But I don't believe there's another man in the country, outside Bearnson and his men, who knows it's there."

"Well, I'll take your word for it, Blaney. If you say the land's open—"

Blaney gave him a long searching look. "You want to buck the Tepee outfit, Than?" He paused to let that thought sink in. "If you're game to do that, there's your land. As pretty a layout as there is north of the Missouri. Just what you want."

Than stared hard at the small blank square where Blaney had set a finger tip. "And you say it's open land?"

"Open as the day. Never been a filing on it. Open so far as the Government is concerned. Closed tight as a drum, so far as old Sam Bearnson has any say-so."

Than had ridden for several big outfits and he knew exactly what cowmen thought of "nesters."

He knew that practice of covering open land, hiding it away within great fenced pastures of their own, so that prospective settlers riding through the country would

12

assume that no land in that vicinity was open to filing. He knew all about their method: Lease of government and Indian land for grazing purposes, script, the illicit hiring of men with homestead rights to file upon certain desirable parcels of land for their boss, who paid all expenses under the guise of wages, and a bonus for the technical sale of the proved claim, when the government requirements had been fulfilled after a fashion.

Just last summer he had been approached; asked to use his land rights for an ambitious wagon boss. It was not timidity but experience which made him pause now.

"What kind of man is this Bearnson?" he wanted to know.

"Oh—all right, I guess. He owns quite a lot of land up in that Broken Hills country. It's common gossip he stands ready to buy claims as fast as they're proved up on, and I'd be willing to bet there ain't a man in the Tepee outfit that's got his homestead right left. If there was, that section up on Running Man wouldn't be open. You can bank on that. Bearnson would be tickled to death to buy you out, if you went in there and proved up."

"We're not figuring on taking up land and then selling out," Than said dryly. "What I'd like to know is, what would happen when he found out we were there to stay?"

Blancy laughed shortly. "Oh, I expect that would settle it," he replied. "The Tepee isn't the shoot-and-grab kind, so far as I know. They run lots of cattle and they need lots of range. Way homesteaders are drifting into the country, they're going to need more. I can't say they'd be tickled to death to see you move in on Running Man. They'll hate like the very devil to see a fence go up along that creek. That land lies just about in

13

the middle of their winter range; the west end, that is. You'll need damn good fences, Than, if you don't want Tepee cattle roosting in your dooryard every time it storms. They hug that timber pretty close in bad weather, I imagine."

"It seems funny they've left land open like that," Than said, still cautious about giving himself to the idea. "How many acres are open? Do you know, Blaney?"

Blaney's mouth tilted up at the corners. "Well, if I didn't know my own district, I'd be a darn poor agent." He drew a pencil from his vest pocket, sprawled as Than had done and lightly outlined the tract without troubling to get a plat of that township. Dickey's eyes widened as they followed the pencil tracing. He had not dreamed that was "covered" land and he had been ten years in that office.

Than, his hat pushed to the back of his head, watched the line extend itself under Blaney's deliberate fingers. "Over a full section!" he cried, when the pencil finally ceased its travels. His brow wrinkled. "More than we can handle. If Sue were older, we could take most of it, but—"

"You don't need her," Blaney stated. "Look here." The pencil dropped again. "Running Man Creek cuts three quarter sections. This, this, and this. You and your mother can take these two dry quarters as desert claims. They're fairly level, as I remember them. They won't cost you much more, and you'll have a nice piece of land among the three of you."

He played absently with the pencil, tapping each end alternately upon the desk beside him. "Let me tell you, Than, I'm superstitious as the devil about some things. Locating land is one."

14

Than looked up at him quickly. "Yeah? How's that?"

"If you want that land, take my advice and file on it *right now*. Not in a week or so, after you've talked it over. *Today*. This forenoon. I've seen it happen dozens of times—there's something uncanny in the way minds seem to leak their intentions so some one gets wise and hops in ahead.

"No use shutting our eyes to it, the Tepee outfit have overlooked a bet here. I suppose they've had this land under fence so long they've kinda forgotten it's open to settlement. Bearnson probably figures it's safe, right in the middle of a ten-section field of his. Dead safe, he thinks. It is, too—till the right man comes along."

Than straightened, banging his fist down upon the map. "Go ahead and fix up the papers, Dickey. I'll get Mother and Dade over here and see what they think about it. If they're game to go in there and buck a cow outfit, we'll file."

CHAPTER THREE

DICKEY CALLED OUT AS THAN WAS HURRYING OUT. "Say, what's your mother's full name? And Dade's, and yours? Think I'm a darned mind reader?"

Than left the door half open. "You can start in on me," he grinned. "Jonathan Emery Roberts, age twenty-five, born in Fort Keogh, Montana (Dad was stationed there; lieutenant—cavalry). Anything else you want to know?"

"Yes. Are you a citizen? And are you black or white?"

"Oh, go to the devil!" Than snorted, and went out, slamming the door behind him.

15

Dickey's yell brought him back as far as the still quivering door. He thrust his head in. "No, I never served a term in the pen, but I might for manslaughter," he stated with ominous import.

"Darn your hide, come in here and shut that door," Dickey commanded, more truculent than his insignificant stature warranted. "Confound it, you seem to think there's nothing to it but to order a homestead same as you'd order a sack of potatoes. There's a little matter of identification of your particular parcel of land. What quarter do you want, you bonehead?"

Than looked at him blankly. "Good glory! How should I know? I never saw the damn place. Blaney, you pick me out a quarter section, will you? And one for Mother and Dade. You got me into this in the first place—go on and fix us up. I'll be back *pronto*, with the folks."

For the third time he departed and this time Dickey let him go.

Blaney kicked his heels against the desk and looked doubtfully at the closed door. "Damn the luck, I wish I'd kept my mouth shut about that Broken Hills land," he said ruefully. "What d'you think about it, Dickey?"

"Search me. What's on your chest, Blaney? Isn't the land any good?"

"Sure, it's good. That's why I spilled the facts the way I did. If I wanted a ranch and had rights enough to cover it, I'd take up every inch of that open land in there on Running Man, and I'd snap my fingers under old Bearnson's nose. But I hate like the devil to send Than down there with his folks. It'll be make or break with them, don't you see? They're selling their home to do it." Blaney scowled at the closed door, seeing only the upper valley on Running Man lying fair, untouched save

16

for the grazing herds of Tepee cattle.

"Well, you aren't responsible for their selling out," Dickey said, breaking the vision as effectively as a dropped stone shatters the mirrored picture in a still pool. "They laid their plans before you knew anything about it. You couldn't stop 'em from taking a bunch of claims, even if you wanted to. I know that old lady; if she's made up her mind—" Dickey threw out both hands and let it go at that.

"Yeah, that's true too. It's having to fight the Tepee outfit—" Blaney turned abruptly toward the little registrar. "Look here, Dickey; you go ahead and make out the papers—but you hold 'em back till Than's had a chance to go down and size up the layout. Then, if they want to file, I'll see 'em through."

"Yeah, that would be lovely, wouldn't it? I've got a picture of me holding up filing papers. Say, I *like* this job! I wouldn't risk it for my wife's pet uncle!" Dickey was carefully removing a shred of lint from his pen point before he wrote Than's name on a filing blank.

Blaney watched him glumly. "I like my job too, but I'd risk it—for Than," he muttered.

Having written "Jonathan Emery Roberts" in the perfectly formed copper-plate lettering which was his one vanity, Dickie looked up. "Don't be so free handing out advice, if you're scared to see it taken," he admonished self-righteously. "Anyway, you say the Tepee's a decent outfit. What are you afraid of?"

Blaney hunched his shoulders, slid off the counter desk and walked over to the nearest window, where he stood looking down over the courthouse lawn. A caretaker was raking off the winter's blanket of mulch, showing the pale green of sprouting grass beneath. Half a dozen glossy-winged blackbirds followed questingly

17

the caretaker's slow progress, snatching hungrily at insects caught off guard.

Through and beyond this scene Blaney saw again the rolling land of the Broken Hills country. "I'd do it myself, if I wanted to homestead," he repeated defensively. "Than could make a mighty fine ranch up there—"

"Let it ride that way," Dickey advised. "Than's able to take care of himself. If it's that cattleman you're thinking of, there isn't a piece of vacant land in the district that a cowman would want to see homesteaded. You know that; at least, that's what you always have told me. Where's that description? Than left it up to you."

Blaney swung about with an impatient movement, passed through the little gate in the railed-off division of the room and went to the file case. He came back with a numbered book of Township Plats and opened it on the desk; turned half a dozen pages with the swift casual manner of long familiarity and picked up his pencil as the pages lay quiet.

"I wish I'd kept my blooming face closed, all the same," he growled, and set his pencil point down upon a certain square. "Give him this quarter for his homestead, and the adjoining one out away from the creek for a desert claim." He lightly checked the two with Than's initials, that there might be no mistake about it.

Dickey peered, made a notation of his own. "Got it," he said briskly.

"All right, put this down for the old lady, adjoining Than, and this for her desert."

"Okay."

"This for Dade, and here's an eighty he could have for his desert." He stood frowning down at the clean

18

white squares. "There isn't a great deal of choice, but as I remember the lay of the land, Than will have the best timber and more of the creek on his homestead. I owe him that much. And Dade, confound him, will get a few clumps of willows and a cottonwood or two."

"You can't make me mad that way," Dickey grinned, while he copied Than's homestead description.

"Than and his mother will have a section together. Dade will be by himself, joining them on the creek, but off to one side where he can't cut in on their land if he flies the track before his time is up."

"You sure do like that feller," Dickey observed slyly.

"Well, I know him to a fare-you-well. He never in his life considered any one but himself, so far as I can discover. If he blows up before he's put in his five years, maybe the girl will be old enough so he can relinquish to her. If he sells out to Bearnson," he added grimly, "I'll take it out of his hide."

"He might not last five years." Dickey was carefully filling in Than's desert filing and spoke only at punctuation points. "Way he's been hitting the booze lately—"

"I hope he straightens up and gets a hold on himself," Blaney filled the pause. "I want to see Than make good down there. He'll need every foot of that land if he wants to raise any cattle at all; and he will, of course—"

A clerk from the city Water Works office came hurriedly in, begging matches. Ten full minutes he remained dawdling there, smoking and talking a great deal about nothing. Blaney wanted to send him back across the hall with the assistance of a boot toe, but he was still lingering when the door opened and Than stood there, holding it while his mother and sister entered.

19

"Well, here we are," Than cheerfully announced, as he followed them in, glancing curiously at the clerk, who sidled out with manifest reluctance. "Dade couldn't get off before six, because tomorrow's pay day and he's up to his eyebrows in work. But he'll come in with me this evening and sign, if that's all right with you. Mother, this is Blaney King. He's a special agent for the government. Dickey you know. Sue, have you met Blaney?"

Blaney took his hands out of his pockets and Dickey sacrificed a freshly lighted cigar. One needn't have looked at Sue Roberts at all but only at the two men, to have known that Sue was a pretty girl.

Yet it was Than's mother who dominated the scene. "What's all this about not wasting a minute to file our homestead rights?" she asked, in a whimsical tone of complaining. "I don't see any crowd here, though you'd have thought the land office was being stormed by an army of land grabbers, the way Thannie hustled us off down here. Tell me, Mr. Agent, what's put the boy into such a fever to sign?"

Dickey grinned and glanced at Blaney, and Blaney explained with a great deal of embarrassment.

"I told you all that, Mom," Than protested, when the facts had been repeated to her. "I said—"

"I know what you said, Jonathan. It's the only land in the State worth having and it's all covered up in a big field. I defy anybody to make any sense of that. If you'll keep still a minute, maybe I can get the straight of the matter. What is it that's covered up, Mr. Blaney?"

"What Than meant is this, Mrs. Roberts. There's a big cattle ranch near there. They don't want homesteaders—nesters, they call them—in there. It would break up their winter range considerably, make it necessary to move two or three miles of fences, and they would lose the use of a mile or so of creek bottom. The fact of the matter is," he added uncomfortably, under her keen scrutiny, "they've got this government land fenced in with a large tract of their own land, lying some distance on both sides of the creek. There is more open land than this in the field, but it's arid for the most part and fit only for grazing."

Still her eyes would not leave his face. "You're a land agent. Did you give them the right to fence in public domain?"

Blaney reddened. "I didn't give them permission," he said. "They'd already done it before I got into the district. I didn't forbid what was already done and make them move their fence. There's lots of vacant land in the country—plenty of it. Unless some one came along who wanted to file on that particular section, the Tepee fence wasn't hurting anything. I know Bearnson pretty well. I've hunted ducks along that creek a couple of seasons and stayed at the ranch."

"So for the sake of a few ducks you'd connive with him—"

"Mother!" Sue protested under her breath.

"No, not that. Bearnson knows I'd never connive to help him keep that land covered, if any one wanted it. I told Than about it, because it's the best location I know of. But of course, there's the Tepee outfit. They may prove something of an obstacle."

"Is it because they want to hang on, that you tried to discourage Thannie—"

"Oh, Mother! Don't be horrid," Sue again interrupted.

"I didn't discourage Than." Blaney stood his ground. "I'd like to see you folks have that section, if you want to file on it. But of course I warned Than of the

21

drawbacks. I wouldn't want to see you have any trouble over it." His mouth tightened. "I'd take it myself, if I wanted to homestead. But I won't advise any one to fight a cow outfit for it."

"Have they any claim to it?"

"No claim whatever." Blaney folded his arms and returned her gaze more steadily. "Any one can go in there tomorrow and start improvements, provided he makes the proper filing, and the law will protect him. The Tepee would have to get their stock off it and keep it off. They'll hate to see it fenced and farmed but there isn't any legal obstacle they could put in your way. If I remember, those claims can be reached without crossing their land; land they hold legally, that is."

Mrs. Roberts looked around at Than and smiled. "I begin to understand your hurry, Jonathan," she said. "It sounds just as tempting as real Irish table linen advertised at half price. But I should like to see the place first." She smiled endearingly at Blaney, who had been half angry at her quizzing. "I always look at the linen," she said. "I pull it and hold it up to the light and chew a thread of the woof before I buy, even if it is only half price."

"I expect to be down that way soon," Blaney ventured. "I could take you and Than up there and show you the place." His eyes nearly stole a glance at Susan as he made the suggestion. "But if you did that, Bearnson would be sure to hear of it and would rush some one in to Chinook to file ahead of you. He isn't asleep, down there. He's stingy enough to hold that land for nothing as long as he thinks it's safe, but he'd spend money fast enough if he thought some one else wanted it."

"What did you say his name is?"

22

"Bearnson. S. P. Bearnson, he signs his name."

"Bearnson. I wonder if he ever ran a store in Helena, away back in the seventies?"

"I haven't the faintest idea." Blaney permitted himself a glance at Susan, who smiled vaguely back at him.

"Bearnson ain't a common name. I'll bet anything it's the same Pete Bearnson!" A gleam showed behind her silver-bowed glasses. She clicked her false teeth and turned to her eldest. "Do you want to go in there and make us a home, Thannie?"

The homestead application made out in his name and ready to sign lay upon the desk at his elbow. Than glanced at it wistfully before he turned his head and smiled down at her. "Just as you say, Mother. Do you think we'd better take a chance, under the circumstances? We may have a fight on our hands."

The gleam had not left her eyes. "I should like to pull it and hold it up to the light first," she complained whimsically. "Still, I *have* bought things from the catalogue without any samples when I knew the firm was reliable." She tilted her head and gave Blaney another measuring look.

"You can bank on that firm, Mother," Than told her with emphasis. "I'd trust Blaney farther than I would my own brother." And he hastened to add, when he saw how that sounded, "We've punched cows together and slept under the same blanket too many times not to know each other."

"I was going to say, Jonathan, that I'm willing to go by the catalogue this time." Her tone put Than in his place. "After all, it isn't just like buying table linen. There's more to it. There's what brought your father and me west in Sixty-five. We took a man's word then and

23

we sold all we had except our health and our hopes—and what we could take in two wagons. Your father drove one and I drove the other. He led two cows behind his wagon and I had a box with six hens and a rooster in mine, and an old cat with three kittens.

"We knew there'd be Indians, most likely, and maybe bears and panthers and wolves; but I learned to use a gun and I kept one loaded and laying in the seat where I could grab it quick. Before ever we started out, I practiced winding the lines around the brake handle and grabbing that gun. I got real good at it. Your father admitted I was quick as a scared cat."

She clicked her teeth again and puckered the leathery skin around her eyes into a hundred deep little wrinkles.

"I guess that cow outfit ain't any worse than Indians," she added humorously. "You go right ahead and sign your application, Thannie, and I'll sign mine. David don't want to a bit, but I'll see to it that he takes all of this land he can get hold of."

She watched Than lean and sign his name wherever Dickey had placed a little cross for him. "We're going by the catalogue, just as your father and I did, when we started west in our two wagons," she said. "I never was sorry for that and I guess I won't be now."

She looked up with a friendly smile for Blaney. "Thannie here was born in a fort, while his father was off with his troops after a band of bad Injuns, and I didn't have a white woman near me; just three or four squaws. But I never was sorry we come west."

She must have seen something of Blaney's worry in his face, for she moved closer and gave his arm a reassuring pat. "Don't you worry a mite," she said. "John and I wouldn't have blamed the man that told us about Montana, if the Indians had skelped us both in our

24

beds; and we sha'n't blame you if we should have to fight old Pete Bearnson for our land.

"I guess gambling ain't all confined to card games and horse racing and Wall Street, and men ain't the only ones that don't like a job any better because it's safe. My land! If I couldn't wonder what was comin' next, I dunno as life would be worth living, hardly. If folks knew what was ahead all the time, there wouldn't be any fun left in making plans and hoping they wouldn't be knocked galley-west. So you just cheer up and don't you worry a minute about us."

Blaney was not an emotional young man, but he came near to taking that stoop-shouldered little old lady in his arms and hugging her as if she were his own mother.

"Thank you," he said simply. "I certainly hope you'll like the place and that you won't have any trouble at all."

"Oh, we don't mind a little trouble now and then," she told him briskly. "Not if it's standing up for our rights. We'll all set more store by our ranch, most likely, if old Pete Bearnson makes a grab or two at it himself."

Dickey asked her name, age and birthplace then, and got the information promptly. Abruptly she turned from Blaney and leaned both gloved hands on the desk beside Than. Her eyes were on Dickey, watching with birdlike intentness while he copied descriptions.

"Dickey Blake, don't you make no mistake in them filing papers," she gave sharp warning. "You dot your i's and cross your t's, young man, and get all them numbers correct. Don't you leave no flaw for Pete Bearnson to lay his finger on and file a contest."

Mother Roberts was a woman who kept her best English, like her best gown, for strangers. Among friends she wore her ungrammatical colloquialisms like a comfortable pair of old shoes. It was a sign of fellowship that she forgot rules now and demanded, "Are you sure them blanks are legal?"

Susan pulled at her mother's sleeve. "Not *them,*" she whispered.

Her mother freed herself with an impatient twitch. "I feel every confidence in your ability, Dickey, and I really have no doubt but what those blanks are the regulation forms authorized by the land office in Washington—but I happen to know Pete Bearnson." She clicked her teeth triumphantly, but otherwise gave no sign that whisper had been heard.

"You bet I'll be careful," Dickey declared. "You sign right there, Mrs. Roberts."

With sudden solemnity, as if she were taking a vow of great portent, the old lady took the pen, leaned and wrote her full name, Susan Elizabeth Roberts, in a finely sloping, old-fashioned hand, her wrinkled lips forming the words as the pen moved over the paper.

"There!—" she exclaimed, standing straight and looking at Blaney with eyes that sparkled behind her glasses. "I feel just as I did over thirty years ago, when we'd loaded in the chickens and the old cat and kittens, and Thannie's father hooked the last tug and handed me the lines. I guess there's a streak of pioneer in me that never will settle down. I'm real excited.

"You pay the fee, Jonathan. And Dickey, you make out David's papers and have 'em all ready. David Jeremiah Roberts, born at Fort Keogh, age twenty-three his next birthday. I'll see to it he signs up this evening and no ifs nor ands about it."

She shook hands with Blaney, told him again that he must not worry a mite, took Susan by the arm and

26

walked grandly from the room, Than following.

Blaney looked wistfully after them. "She's the old pioneer stock," he mused. "It's women like her that helped make this country what it is today. She's worth a dozen ordinary men, Dickey. I guess I needn't worry about Than. He'll make a go of it—with those two women."

Susan was a pretty girl, of the kind to haunt a man's dreams. Nevertheless, the thoughts of the two left in the land office lingered with the little old lady who had come west in Sixty-five.

CHAPTER FOUR

ON HIS WAY HOME FROM THE MEAT COMPANY'S OFFICE that evening, Dade left the rough plank sidewalks of First Avenue North and walked the short length of concrete pavement to the courthouse. Inside the plate-glass door, Than stood waiting.

Dade's lip curled. "Afraid I wouldn't come?" he taunted. "You needn't be alarmed. I intend to let you folks go ahead and make fools of yourselves. When you get a bellyful of homesteading, you'll maybe admit I was right." He coughed.

"Maybe you'll be the one to admit we had the right idea," Than shot back at him, as they fell into step down the long echoing corridor, "when you quit barking and get some meat on your ribs."

Dade stopped short in his nervous stride. A flush stained his cheekbones. "Say, if you folks have got the notion you have to do this for my health—" he coughed again rackingly, "I'll turn around right now. I'm tired of being coddled and babied. I'm able to take care of

27

myself."

"Don't make a damned fool of yourself," Than cut in. "Mom's made up her mind she wants a ranch. The mere fact that summer in the open air will cure that cough of yours ain't what I'd call a drawback. Of course," he added with brotherly sarcasm, "if you want to hang onto it, I guess there's no law against your living in a dugout and poisoning yourself with all the bad air you want."

"Poppycock!" snarled Dade. But he went on in and signed the papers Dickey had made ready.

When he had finished, he looked up and lowered a supercilious eyelid. "Bats in the family belfry," he jibed. "Chorus of mixed voices singing, 'That little old sod shanty on my claim.' They'll soon get enough of that."

"What're you doing it for?" bantered Dickey, who very well knew.

Dade waved a slim, soft, bookkeeper's hand. "Three against one. It'll be almost worth it, just being there to watch the show when they come out of their pipe dream."

Again it was Than who paid the fee. He followed Dade out, angrily wondering why the whole family should transplant itself to the wilderness for the sake of an ungrateful young hound like Dade. For the time it took to walk the six blocks home, Than reflected bitterly that Dade was not worth the sacrifice his mother was making; that Dade was going to be their biggest handicap, and that if it were possible, he would go back and tear up those filing papers and let Dade go to the devil; that he'd rather fight all the cowmen in the country than put up with any more of Dade's lip.

His angry meditations brought them to their own green-painted gate. He walked stiff-backed through it and let it swing against Dade's legs, and never looked

28

back or offered the slightest apology. That Dade offered no insult in return only made him the angrier. While he made ready for supper, he reminded himself of nearly every one of Dade's shortcomings. But it is well known that brother can be terribly enraged with brother and nothing come of it. When he entered the cramped little dining room, somehow Than forgot his indignation.

Dade was standing with one arm around his mother's shoulders and he was gently tweaking her ringed ear while he made ridiculous threats in a deep villainous tone.

"For the third and last time, do I get peach preserves? You'd better disgorge." His voice dropped to a more ominous note. "I'll keep hogs; trained hogs. The mean, diggy kind. I'll chase them up to your place and make them root up your garden. Peach preserves—to go with those hot biscuits in the oven. Yes or no?"

"No. David, if you don't behave yourself—"

"Ugh—ugh," David grunted realistically. "Spotted hogs with long snouts. You won't have a radish or an onion or a cabbage to your name, old lady. Your claim will be swarming with hogs. My hogs."

"I'll keep a pack of bloodhounds and I'll sic them onto your hogs." Mother Roberts was playing the game, mouth puckered tight against a smile, eyes glaring through her spectacles.

"I'll train my hogs to lick your hounds. They'll go ki-yi-ing home and crawl under your dugout" (he shot a quizzical glance at Than) "every time they see a hog of mine come trotting over the hill."

"Your hogs'll run all their fat off, gettin' home with their ears chawed. You can't have any p'serves and you might just as well quit actin' up. I've only got one jar left and I'm savin' that for when the Ladies' Aid meets

29

here next week."

"So! Old woman, you'd take the preserves from your children's mouths and cast them before the Ladies' Aid! I'll keep hogs and—" leaning to peer gloatingly into her face "—I'll keep—*goats*!"

"There's good fresh honey—"

"Goats that will stand on the roof of your little old sod shanty and say '*Baa-aa*!' down your stovepipe. They'll stomp their feet and rattle clods down into your coffee—"

"Oh, for pity's sake, do be quiet! I'm going to have a log house—"

"Goats that will butt and baa-aa you every time you poke your head out—"

"I'd oughta turn you across my apron and spank you good! You're letting the supper get all cold. You let go of me this minute, or—"

"Peach preserves—goats—one or the other. Which'll it be? Honey makes me sick." The play ended suddenly in a coughing fit. Dade let go of her, retreated to the kitchen porch. The distressing sound of his continued coughing came raspingly through the closed door.

"Go get them p'serves, Babe." A look of pain and infinite tenderness swept over Dade's mother. "I guess they'll do us as much good as they will the Ladies' Aid. My land, I wish we could pack up and get out onto them claims tomorrow. The boy'll cough himself to death if something ain't done pretty quick." She turned to Susan, standing inquiringly in the doorway, with a glass jar of rich golden fruit in her two slim hands. "Dish 'em up in them cut-glass sauce dishes, Baby. Dade likes that star pattern so." She caught Than's eyes upon her and a defensively tight look crept around her mouth. "Them's the dishes I'd use for the Ladies' Aid and I guess my own folks are as good as they be."

"Sure hope so," Than replied to the glance she gave him. "You've got the right idea, Mom." But behind all that he wondered why she felt impelled to explain. He and Susan took it for granted that Dade would get what he wanted. He always had and he always would.

"How soon do you think we can get onto our land, Thannie? Mr. Murchison says the deed to this place'll be all made out and ready to sign tomorrow, and the money'll be in the bank ready to pay right over. I sh'd think we might begin packin' up right away, ready to move."

"You'll want a place to move into, Mom," Than pointed out. "If this weather holds, I can probably get some kind of shack built inside a month—"

Than stopped. His mother was not listening. Dade had returned to the dining room, looking, pale and exhausted, tiny beads of moisture on brow and cheeks. A vein in his temple next Than was beating noticeably. His mother's eyes were dim and shadowed with worry as Than held her chair for her, but she sat down briskly and harked back to her pretended quarrel.

"I can't have goats trompin' around on my roof," she complained, "so I made up my mind I better give in and let you have the p'serves." Her withered hands moved deftly, filling the top plate of the four piled in front of the browned roast with its ring of halved potatoes. She was choosing the best for Dade, as a matter of course.

"Thannie says he'll start in right away, building a cabin for us to move into," she said with resolute cheerfulness, as she handed the plate to Dade. "Seems to me I can't wait to get there. If we can get a patch ploughed up right away, we can raise a good garden this summer."

31

"For my hogs," Dade said huskily but with a sly glance at his mother. He drank thirstily of the strong black coffee she interrupted her serving to pour for him, and a little color came back into his face. "That's the only legitimate reason I can see for this sudden desire to go hew yourself a home out of the wilderness," he went on in the carping tone his family knew so well.

"Now, David, I've got lots of good reasons for wanting us to use our homestead rights. In a few years all the good land will be taken up and we'd have our rights on our hands with nothing to show for them." She passed Than his plate with a hand not quite steady. "I don't believe in letting valuable things go to waste," she said primly.

"Poppycock," Dade retorted impatiently. "I'll bet you've got some granny notion about my health. What did that fool doctor stuff into your head? He put you up to this land craze, now, didn't he?"

Mother Roberts caught a quick breath and laid down her carving knife. "David Jeremiah Roberts, don't give me any of your impudence, or I'll have Babe take them peach p'serves off the table this minute! Doctor Gordon said the very thing I've been ding-donging you about all winter. He said you shouldn't run around with your overcoat off—or else unbuttoned half the time. He's seen you times enough, and he said these cold winds keep that ticklin' in your throat from gettin' any better. I've been at you to wear a muffler and keep your chest covered up, and he says the same thing. He told me you're just askin' for a spell of pneumonia, first time you get your feet wet." She went back to slicing a thin piece of roast for herself. "And you better heed what we both tell you or you'll be down sick," she climaxed her scolding.

Dade was not satisfied. He looked suspiciously from under his brows at Than, then back to his mother. "That all he said?" His eyes scrutinized her face.

"Well, for pity's sake! Ain't that enough? What more could he say? A ticklin' cough like that ain't to be fooled with just because it don't amount to much. If you go out to-night, you take your muffler, young man, and *you wear it*. Them's his orders and I back 'em up."

"Sure he didn't give you a song and dance about galloping consumption or some such tommyrot, and scare you into pulling up stakes here?"

"Consumption?" His mother achieved a shocked incredulous look. "Consumption of food, maybe, and gallopin' up to the table. You needn't to think, David, that cough of yours is goin' to bamboozle anybody into thinkin' it might be consumption. My land! I've had a ticklin' cough like yours months on end, when I was doin' all my own washin' and had to hang out clothes in all kinds of weather. I kept my throat raw every winter, coughin'. Way I used to spit up blood, a body that didn't know might think I was in the last stages."

"You may think you're fooling me," Dade said querulously. "There's something back of this sudden enthusiasm for homesteading. I just want to say that if it's on my account you're doing it, you might just as well calm down and tell that little runt of a Dick Blake to tear up those applications."

"The very idea!" gasped Mother Roberts. "I won't do no such a thing! If I want to prove up on a homestead, I'm going to. This is my place, to do with as I'm a mind to. I been dickering with Murchison long before I ever took you to see a doctor. I've sold out, David, and even if I could back down, I wouldn't do it. I've used the homestead right your father left me, and I've took me

33

up a claim like I always wanted to do. If you ain't man enough to stand by your old mother and help make improvements on a ranch, Babe and I'll go alone. There ain't any Pete Bearnson goin' to grab up land that don't belong to him and hang onto it—not while I've got a homestead right to use on it, Babe and I'll go ahead—"

"Moses!" gasped Dade. "Now we're getting down to facts. So you've got a chance to fight somebody, is that it? Who is this said Pete Bearnson? Than never mentioned him."

"Pete Bearnson's a man I've been waitin' twenty years to learn a lesson to," snapped Mrs. Roberts. "He's a mean old skinflint that'd ruther rob widows and orphans than eat. I always said I'd live to see him get his come-uppance, and I will, too."

Dade cleaned his preserve dish without realizing what it was he was eating. "Than, what's all this about? You know anything about this feud of Mom's?"

"Not until today," Than replied as indifferently as he dared. "Some old flame of Mom's has got our claims fenced in with his own land, according to Blaney King––and if he don't know, nobody does." Than studiously stirred his coffee. Of course, Mom was putting up any argument that would convince Dade this hegira had nothing to do with his health. She didn't realize that she had twice failed to mention her son Jonathan as a factor in the scheme; or maybe she was afraid of stirring Dade's jealousy. All the same, that little omission hurt.

On the pretext that he must look after Black Hawk, he excused himself from the table and left the house. Their voices followed him down the steps. He was gone some time, and when he returned Dade was still there and he was talking about hogs. On the table before them lay Susan's latest geography, open at the map of Montana,

34

and Dade was gravely using the scale of miles and his lead pencil for a measuring stick, making an estimate of the distance he would have to haul his hogs to market.

"That's too far," his mother was saying. "In the fall of the year's when you'd want to do your shippin', and that's the time when the weather's tricky. I most believe, David, we'd better figure on raising a few cattle or sheep. You could drive them out to the railroad—but you never in this world could drive hogs."

"Pork," said Dade wisely, "is steadier in the market than any other meat—and higher. Pork is an economic necessity—"

"Well, good land!" Than heard his mother's teeth click. "Ain't beef, I'd like to know?"

"Not so much as pork. You take ham, bacon, salt pork—we could butcher and cure our own meat. I know how it's done."

"You'd have to have corn, David, and I don't believe that's a corn country."

"Why corn? The Company keeps a big drove of hogs on its ranch out in the Highwoods, and they don't feed corn—"

"You need corncobs for smokin' hams and bacon," his mother made tart rejoinder. "I guess I ought to know. I may not run a butcher shop nor keep books in one, for that matter—but I've smoked enough meat in my time. It's a country just made for cows, David. Or sheep—"

"They'd run you out, if you took in sheep."

"I'd like to see old Pete Bearnson try runnin' me out! For half a cent, I'd buy me some sheep just to spite him. A body could sell the wool in the spring and the wethers in the fall—"

Than gave a short laugh and went on into the living

35

room where Susan was playing Lange's "Flower Song" with deft fingers, while her attention was divided between the clock and the doorbell. She had on her hat and coat and Than thought some fellow was sure lucky that night. Susan sent him a detached smile over her shoulder and Than went on into the hall and picked up the telephone directory. Maybe he could find Blaney. Dickey would know where to get him. He wanted to talk about his homestead, make plans with some one, as Dade and his mother were doing. They didn't feel the need of him, he could see that. Nothing new, but nevertheless it hurt. Babe had her beau—she didn't need him, either.

Than threw down the directory, slid his arms into his overcoat and went out, around the house and back to the stable. Hawk nickered softly when he opened the door.

He had saddled and was leading the black horse outside when a horseman loomed silently beside the corral gate.

"That you, Than? I got to thinking about those filings. Hoped I'd catch you at home so I could have a talk with you. Going somewhere?"

Blaney! Than's mood lifted. In the bright starlight Blaney saw his smile.

"Yeah, I was just starting out to hunt you up."

"Anything wrong?" Blaney leaned forward as Than closed the gate on Hawk's rump. "Dade bucking the idea? I heard he was pretty nasty in the office this evening."

"No, he's in the house, going round and round with Mom over hogs, sheep or cattle." Than swung a leg over the cantle, reined Hawk up alongside Blaney so that his right stirrup touched Blaney's left with a dull clinking sound. "Dade'll go ahead now, like it was his own idea in the first place. You know Dade."

"Yeah, I know Dade!" Blaney hunched his shoulders. They turned into the quiet, tree-shadowed avenue, instinctively riding toward the open land beyond the river.

CHAPTER FIVE

Snow came to warn them that even the meadowlarks could make a mistake. Then bitter winds that lifted the light snowfall and sent it swirling through streets emptied of people. Dade's cough became alarmingly worse. He developed a temperature that kept him away from the office for days.

"You might just as well quit and be done with it," his mother declared, in the scolding tone she used to hide her worry. "You and Jonathan will have to get started building our cabins, just as quick as it warms up again. This is the real breakup of winter. We've got to give possession of this place in a month and by that time—"

"What if it storms for a month?" Dade's voice was husky, his temper brittle. "We'll have to get out in a blizzard, I suppose. That's a woman's management for you!"

"You needn't to talk like that to me, David. This storm won't last. And the law only gives a homesteader just so long to get onto his claim, remember. Thannie's off lookin' at work horses. You boys are goin' to need a good strong team apiece, besides your saddle horses. And I've promised Babe she should have a horse to ride, so there's six horses to be bought. Soon as you git over this cold of yours, you could be lookin' at machinery. Jonathan's busy every minute of the day,

37

and soon as you're able, it's your place to help him get things together so you boys can get started." And Dade never knew it was her frantic haste to get him out of town that made her such a driving force in the family.

Than was indeed busy every minute. Yet, because of storms and Dade's illness, March had made way for April before the start was made. Then, one morning at daybreak, Than drove a loaded four-horse wagon around to the little green gate on Fourth Avenue North. Susan came running out to give her little gray saddle horse a goodbye lump of sugar, and Mother Roberts, with her arms full of things remembered at the last minute, followed close behind.

"David will be right out," she said hurriedly, as she handed up a gray blanket and a can of fresh doughnuts. "You watch him, Thannie. He's awful touchy, but you be patient. The doctor thinks this is the best thing in the world for him, but he says it will take time, and we'll have to watch David and not let him overdo. You drive slow and take it easy till you see how he stands it, won't you, Jonathan?"

"You bet. Don't you worry, Mom. I'll look after him like a daddy."

"But don't let on, whatever you do," she warned him anxiously. "If he once suspicioned it's on his account we're goin', he'd turn on us like a wolf, and we couldn't do a thing for him. So you be tactful and patient, Thannie, won't you? The doctor says—"

"Here he comes," Than warned under his breath, then spoke in his usual tone. "You bet, Mom, we'll drop you a card from every town we strike. Dade'll do that. He's the pen-pusher of the outfit."

"Of course I'll write," Dade said testily, as he came through the gate, buttoning his long coat of unplucked

38

beaver. "You folks better get back into the house. You'll freeze out here."

"It's a fine-lookin' outfit," Mother Roberts said wistfully, as her glance roved from the arched neck of the two big brown mares in the lead to the tarp-covered wagon loaded with camp outfit; and to the two saddle horses tied behind. Black Hawk, saddled and with his reins tied to the saddle horn, was left loose. He would follow like a dog.

"I wish I were going along," Susan said forlornly. "Can't I, Mom?"

"Say, if we don't get started *pronto*, you'll both be trying to hang on behind," Than bantered. From the corner of his eye he watched his mother and Dade; saw how she clung at the last moment, saw too how Dade let his lips brush past her cheek, not wanting to kiss her. With Babe it was the same; a perfunctory make-believe caress. Say what he might, Dade knew what dread malady had set its fangs upon him; he knew and he was trying not to let the others suspect.

A stab of pity caught Than by the throat. He spread the gray blanket, tucked one side around his legs, left more than half for Dade. "Well goodbye—be good to yourselves!" he called out with a false hilarity, and gathered up the reins. The leaders threw up their heads, leaning against the collars. The heavy load moved, the two led horses jumped as the lead ropes tightened suddenly. Black Hawk kicked up his heels and broke into a trot. Dade turned himself half about on the high spring seat, looked back and lifted his hand in a half salute as the outfit went chuckling away up the street in the frosty air, straight toward the red dawn glowing behind the bare tree branches with their swollen buds waiting for another warm day.

East to where a street turned down to Black Eagle bridge. Clattering across, the four sleek horses flinching at the hollow sound of their hoofbeats, leaning together across the tongue and chain, afraid of the humming vibration in cable and steel rod. Than's spirit lifted to meet the chill dawn wind plucking at gray hatbrim as it whistled down over the river. He wanted to whoop, to sing at the top of his lusty young voice. Only for Dade, bundled in his beaver coat, he would have done it. No more riding across to the barren hills beyond the smelter, galloping like one hunted away from town, knowing he must presently turn and gallop back again. This time he was free to go on and on along the brown trail, and never turn back.

Today he exulted, because he didn't know what lay ahead along the trail; what trials, what adventures, what hopes or—perhaps—what happiness. Past the smelter spewing its unending yellowish-green garland of smoke to go streaming away before the wind. Up the steep, smoke-blackened hill on the road he knew so well. Past the hollow where the meadowlark first told him it was spring and woke his sleeping hunger for the range. Down a hill, his right foot braced against the brake, the wheelers leaning backward, breeching straps pressed deep into their glossy brown rumps; up the steep slope to another crest, all four horses digging in their toes, pulling true and even, with straightened backs, collars creaking softly as they took the strain. Good horses, these. They'd pull till they dropped.

The wind did not lessen as the sun rose. It blew chill from the northwest, roughening the hair on the horses' rumps, whipping their tails out over the right tugs, tossing their heavy manes. The gray blanket rippled over the knees of the two, puffed up as the wind found a

40

way under.

Than leaned, caught a corner flapping loose, tucked it tight and snug. He gave a sidewise glance at Dade. "Cold?"

Dade shook his head, the impatient negative gesture Than knew so well. "I'm all right," he said shortly. His tone sounded repressed, as if he were holding back a coughing spell.

Best let Dade alone and not make him talk. Than gave himself up to the wide-flung distances, to the four horses forging steadfastly farther and farther up the brown trail, to the led horses already learning to keep their lead ropes slack, to Black Hawk trotting along behind, with empty stirrups swinging.

On the evening of the fifth day, with the clouds hanging low and promising rain, they pulled thankfully into Camas, which was the town nearest to their land. And there, when they entered the one small saloon which was also the office and lobby of the one small hotel, they spied Blaney King behind a small table, playing seven-up with a big-hatted range man. He was sitting facing the door and Than felt an intangible load slip from his mind as their eyes met. Blaney excused himself to his companion and came forward. Than caught a stinging slap on his shoulder.

"Hello, Than. Just pull in?" Blaney greeted.

"Yeah. Just stopped to see if we can get a room in this shebang, before I hunt a place to set up the tent." The bartender stood waiting to perform his duty as hotel clerk, and Than grinned as he moved on to the desk. "And what the devil are you doing here?" he added to Blaney, as he picked up an ink-incrusted pen and looked at it, abstractedly wondering whether it would make a mark.

"I? Oh, thunder, man, I chase all over the country, regardless. That's what Uncle Sam pays me for." Blaney's voice slid into complaining. "Say, I've been hunting this place from one end to the other, looking for some one who can play a decent game of billiards. Come on, you highbinder. We'll just about have time for a game before our supper."

It was a subtle warning to keep their meeting one of casual friendliness. Than nodded understandingly while he wrote his name and Dade's on the dog-eared register.

"I've got to take care of our outfit. Ask Dade. He hasn't been doing anything but sit on a high seat and let his legs hang down."

Blaney glanced at Dade. "How about it?" In spite of himself, his tone was perfunctory.

Dade shook his head, with the faint one-sided smile that was a trick of his and gave an air of condescension to his words. "If you'll bring the table over here by the stove and warm a cue for me, and find me a good man to use it, I might play." He spread his thin white hands to the heat and gave a dry hacking cough.

Blaney looked from one to the other, gave a snort of pretended disgust. "Oh, all right, if you feel that way about it. Say, Than, want me to show you where I always put up my horse when I'm in town?"

"Yeah, sure. And I want to show you the best pulling team in the State." Than started for the door. "Better come bring in our grips, Dade."

They were driving away when Than looked inquiringly at Blaney. "What's up?"

"Not a great deal. I just thought it might help some if I served notice I'm a friend of yours. Funny—I was in Chinook a week or so ago and I found out something. Four different fellows have showed up at the land office there in the last two or three weeks and wanted to file on those claims of yours. Looks to me like Bearnson smelled a rat, but I don't see how."

Than gave him a startled look. "They didn't *file*?"

"Lord, no! How could they? I traced them down; one is working for the Tepee now and the other used to. The other two took up land just outside the Tepee field. They'll be neighbors of yours. What struck me as odd was the fact they suddenly came to life and wanted in on that particular tract. That office don't get more than two or three filings a month. Bearnson's worried, all right."

"That'll tickle Mom."

"Yeah—swing in here. Stable's right up this little lane. Don't let on I said anything, will you, Than? I'm not supposed to butt in or take sides, except where the land laws are being evaded. There's no law against wanting to file a claim. I just thought I'd tell yuh."

"Well, thanks. Kinda looks as though we wouldn't be any too welcome around this neck of the woods."

"Well, those two homesteaders on Dry Creek may give you the bad eye at first, but there's a full section between your claims, so that ought to prevent any squabbling. I thought maybe I'd better tell you, Than; just in case."

"Glad you did, Blaney. Gives me a line on things. Say, I hope it isn't fixing to rain. What d' you think?"

Blaney studied the low-hanging clouds. "I'd hate to bet it won't. If the wind changes, though, it will probably clear off. How did Dade stand the trip? Looks pretty peaked, to me."

"Why, all right, I guess. I don't see much difference in him, one way or the other. Dade never does open up to me, though. Mom's about the only one he'll really

43

talk to."

The stableman came out, then, and Blaney introduced Than. "Friend of mine. We used to ride together long ago, before we started shaving. Say, can't we run the wagon inside?"

Certainly they could. The stableman hastened to slide back the big doors. "Just in case," Blaney muttered, as Than reined the leaders around to make the turn.

"Say, I'm sure glad you happened to be in town," Than said, when they were walking in the dusk back to the hotel. "That's what I call luck."

"Yeah, I'm glad it happened this way too," Blaney replied with convincing carelessness. "Of course, I travel all over the country; been over in Valley County––" Without seeming to do so, he turned the subject into another channel, and even Than, who knew him better than he knew his own brother, never dreamed that Blaney had kept himself well informed of their movements, knew when they left home and had timed his own visit to Camas accordingly; or that Blaney had waited two full days for this meeting which seemed so purely accidental.

He was mildly astonished—but still not suspicious—when he drove up to the hotel for Dade and the grips next morning and found Blaney standing on the porch, buttoning his slicker. His big, deep-chested roan horse stood with a blanket thrown over the saddle and reins tied to the corner post, blinking the rain from his eyelashes.

"Good glory!" Than exclaimed. "You must have urgent business this morning, Blaney. I'd think you'd keep under cover."

"Say, I don't earn my salary staying in outa the rain," Blaney retorted. "I happen to be riding up your way, so

I thought I might as well trail along, if you don't mind."

"Sure you ain't going outa your way?"

"Absolutely. This isn't going to break into my plans a darned bit." Which was perfectly true, since this was his plan.

"Say, I hate to call you a liar—"

"Then don't. By the way, did you fellows think about getting a lunch put up? There's a stretch of dobe that'll make damned heavy going in this rain. We'll be lucky if we make the claims by dark."

"*We?*"

Blaney chuckled. "Well, you'd have a deuce of a time finding your claims without me, especially if you bumped into any of the Tepee outfit and they got chesty with you."

Dade, going back after a lunch, gave Blaney a hard stare as he passed. Blaney wondered what was in his mind, but he said nothing. He went down the steps, walked around the wagon, inspected the tarp fastenings.

"Pretty snug load," he made approving comment. "Hope this darn rain lets up."

A vain hope it proved to be. All day they drove slowly over the drenched hills and into muddy coulees, Blaney on his big roan piloting the way. Afternoon waned dismally while they toiled to the top of a long, rutted slope. At the first level, where the trail turned sharply to avoid a hill too steep to climb, Than pulled up and set the brake to give the rain-roughened, steaming horses a breathing spell. Blaney turned and rode back, dismounting beside the wagon.

"Better let me drive, from here on," he said. "We'll take a short cut through the Tepee field. It'll be rough as the devil but we can cut off over five miles of bad trail. Hunch over, will you, Than?"

45

Than surrendered the lines, thrust his chilled hands deep into his pockets. Blaney settled himself on the high spring seat, kicked off the brake and swung the leaders sharply to the right. Down a steep, grassy swale he drove, brake grinding hard. Half a mile along the level, bumping over scattered stones. A four-wire fence barred the way. Blaney got down, found a stone and knocked the staples out of three posts. He weighted the wires with rocks laid across them, climbed in and picked up the lines.

Without a word he drove through. They were trespassing on Tepee land.

CHAPTER SIX

A MEADOWLARK CLOSE BY WOKE THAN FROM THE dreamless sleep of a man healthily tired. He lay blinking at the tent roof, for a minute or two not quite remembering where he was or why he was there. On round-up, he thought at first; but there should be a stir of men and horses to waken the birds. Then, as memory snapped into gear, his face relaxed into a half-smile of deep content. He was in his own tent, camped beside his own creek, and that was his own meadowlark singing; his as much as any man's on earth. With an unlooked-for surge of emotion he thrilled to the consciousness of ownership, to the realization that for the first time in his whole life he had slept on his own individual property; his unless by his own acts he forfeited the right to claim it.

Dade and Blaney were still asleep. Dade would probably be the first to awaken, roused by the terrific spell of coughing that tormented him every morning. Hot coffee always helped. Than sat up carefully so as not to disturb Blaney, who slept beside him, and reached stealthily for his clothes. He was out of the tent without having made a sound, gazing around him, face alight with something more than the dawn.

It was just as Blaney had described it, he was thinking exultantly. High wooded hills to the west and to the eastward the gently sloping valley. The wagon and the hurriedly erected tent stood close to the creek he knew was Running Man. Hipshot under their sodden blankets, the horses stood tied to the unloaded wagon, wisps of baled hay scattered on the ground. As the light strengthened, Than could see the faint green of bursting leaf buds on the scattered trees near by. Here and there sturdy pine trees stood. High amongst the topmost branches of the nearest pine, a bird called sharply. Down by the creek the meadowlark answered with its short, sweet ripple of melody.

Than drew a long, deep breath. With a final slow glance that swept from hilltops to the valley below, he turned to the problem of finding dry wood. Everything was drenched from the rain, but a low-branched pine tree sheltered cones gummy with pitch. A little farther back in the grove stood a lightning-blasted tree where the pitch had hardened in amber ridges along great splinters torn from the tree's very heart. These he gathered, coming into camp with an armload of splinters and dragging a dry branch behind him, his own wood, culled from his grove, he reminded himself. Blaney had said last night that they were camped somewhere near the center of Than's homestead. As he threw down the wood and straightened to gaze once more around the peaceful scene, he heard a chuckle behind him.

"Monarch of all you survey." Blaney said, coming up beside him and laying a hand none too gently on his shoulder. "Only you're not. You're surveying the upper end of your mother's homestead, if I remember correctly.

"I always used to think that a house ought to stand right here, Than; or maybe over there by that pine. Four o'clocks in the front yard, hens clucking around in the back—see what I mean?"

"Good glory, yes! I should say I do. I've got that house all built. I was just starting to put up a corral and stable down there on that knoll, with the corral sloping down to the creek bank; or close enough so I could run water in a ditch—"

"Say, there's a spring right over there by that big cottonwood; right in that outcropping of rock. You can see the top of the currant bushes from here. Your east line runs just the other side of that bend, I believe. How long will it be before we eat? I think I'll just walk down around there and locate your corner. Won't take over half an hour."

"That'll be just about right for breakfast," Than declared, opening his knife to whittle shavings from a splinter heavy with pitch.

"I'll be back," Blaney called over his shoulder, as he strode away down the creek.

Than started a fire, filled the coffeepot at the creek, added coffee and set it on a flat rock close to the blaze. He fed the horses a quart of oats apiece, pulled off two flakes of hay from the bale he had opened for their supper, divided it among the eight.

He was turning rashers of bacon in the frying pan, a basin of bannock batter on the grass beside him ready to go into the pan when the bacon was out, when two horsemen came loping down the slope, following the wagon tracks to the creek. Than gave them a long

48

glance and turned back to his bacon. He did not look up again until the riders drew rein as close as their horses would stand beside the fire.

Than stood up, a guarded smile easing the cool appraisal of his eyes. "Howdy, boys. You're riding early."

One, a tall young fellow with engraved silver conchos on his chaps, took his eyes off the wagon and horses and looked at Than. He spat reflectively into the grass.

"Yeah. Kinda early. Been trailin' skunks."

"You have?" Than bent to his bacon frying again. "Any luck?"

"Well, we located one, anyway." The tall rider suddenly abandoned the metaphor. "Kinda helpin' yourself, ain't yuh? Makin' yourself pretty damn much at home, seems to me."

"Hope to tell you I am." Than reached for a tin plate, lifted the frying pan from the fire and began taking up the bacon.

"I don't s'pose you saw that fence back there a mile or so, did yuh? Just laid down the wires kinda absent-minded like and drove right through? Mere fact that you were goin' where you got no business didn't bother you a damn bit, did it?"

"Not a damn bit," Than agreed.

"Then it won't bother you none to hitch onto that wagon and make tracks outa this field." The cowboy's tone was no louder, but his words came out with the snap of a whip. "And make it now," he added grimly. "Kick that fire apart and get busy. You got ten minutes to hitch up and throw your stuff back on the wagon. Move, damn yuh! We can't waste no time on yuh. We got work to do."

"You sure have," Than agreed again, pouring

49

bannock batter into the hot grease evenly and to just the right thickness. "You've sure got plenty work all cut out for you, because I expect to be here a long, long while."

"You what? Why, you blank blank blankety-blank—"

Than moved his sizzling bannock from the fire to a box near by and stood up. "Say, you get down off your horse before you go any farther," he snapped. "That is, if you aren't scared to."

"Scared? Me? Why, you gee-damned, longeared this and that—"

"Pile off—before I drag you off!" Than was shedding his coat. "I don't know who you are and I don't give a damn. But I know damn well you'll go off draggin' a hind leg, you blinkety-blink bing-bing-bang!"

"Pile in! Lick 'im, Dilly, or I will m'self," yelped the little fellow on the big gray. "He's twice as big as I am, but by Harry, I'll do it!"

"You shut up!" Dilly commanded shortly. "Hold my horse a minute." He swung a long and limber leg over the cantle and came down in a hurry, handing the reins to the small cowboy.

"Over here." Than backed to a spot well away from fire and guy ropes, and the tall puncher, waiting only to pull off his coat and spurs and hang them on the saddle, rushed after him, eager for the fray.

"Better shuck your chaps," Than jibed. "You're liable to dent those fancy conchos of yours!"

"You'll be worse'n dented!" The one called Dilly retorted through closed teeth, and lifted his fists as he danced in like a boxer.

"Tie into 'im, Dilly! Knock his damn block off, why don'tcha?"

"Aw, dry up!" Dilly shouted roughly and got a smack on the jaw when he wasn't looking for it.

The jar brought him up short. He ducked, came up suddenly and swung his long arm in a downward arc that Than stopped with his big hat, which jammed down over his eyes.

While the little fellow on the gray horse chortled with glee, the tall man took savage advantage of Than's mishap.

Than caught two rocking blows while he yanked off his hat and sent it spinning toward the tent. The man Dilly grinned ominously, sent his own hat sailing after Than's, and the two went at it in dead earnest.

They sparred, dodged, struck and parried and struck again, fighting furiously. They clinched, stood swaying and straining together, each taking the other's hot breath. Than it was who tripped the cowboy, landed on top of him and had his own face rubbed into the rain-soaked grass when a terrific bear hug caught him unaware. He kicked, struggled, felt the breath being relentlessly forced out of his lungs, as with a last desperate effort he heaved the cowboy half over and broke that iron embrace.

For half a minute they lay there gasping, too weak to fight yet afraid to let go. Dark hazel eyes glared into eyes of flashing blue. Breath of rage from their flaring nostrils met and mingled. Clenched teeth bared in sardonic grins.

"You damned—sheep herder!" panted the cowboy, when he could speak. "I'll—bust you—wide open!"

"Fly at it—why don'tcha? You damned—knot-head–"

"Oh—ah—just a minute!" Blaney's voice sounded calm above them. "Dilly, I want you to meet my friend, Than Roberts. Than, meet John Dillebrandt; Dilly for short."

51

Arms suddenly relaxed, they rolled apart and sat up drunkenly swaying.

"Yeah—I been meetin' your friend," Dillebrandt said dryly, and cautiously fingered a cut and swelling underlip. "Where-all you annex a catamount like him?"

"Now don't let me interrupt," Blaney hurried to add. "I just thought maybe you fellows might like to know who you're trying to take apart."

"Good glory!" Than grinned wryly as he staggered to his feet and drew a sleeve across his face, wincing as it touched certain raw places. "We were just beginning to find out."

They stood eyeing each other dubiously, neither wanting to make the first move, until Than caught a twinkle in the cowboy's eyes.

"I always did hate to fight on an empty stomach," Than said then, moving toward the fire and his neglected bannock. "Blaney, if you feel like explaining how we happen to be here, I'll go ahead and finish breakfast. We can fight it out afterwards."

"Not on your life!" Dillebrandt called over his shoulder and turned an inquiring glance upon Blaney. "I sure am surprised to see you here, Mr. King. Ducks ain't ripe yet."

Blaney chuckled. "Well, that gives me an excuse to come back later." His voice and manner became more formal. "This is just a little side trip for me. I happened to be in Camas, yesterday, when the Roberts boys pulled in. Other one isn't up yet, I guess. Than, here, I've known since Hector was a pup. In fact, we started bravely out when we'd oughta been wearing knee pants still, and got a job on round-up. We—say, how long was it we punched cows together, Than?"

"About four years," Than looked up from his bannock

frying to reply. "Four spring round-ups and three in the fall. Last beef round-up we worked together, you were sent on with a trainload of cattle and you never did show up, after that."

Blaney laughed. "That's right. I fell by the wayside; got tangled up with the land office." He looked at Dillebrandt. "So you see, Dilly, Than and I are kinda old hands together. And it seems he and his folks have filed on some land in here, so I came on out to show Than where it lies."

"Oh. So that's it, hunh? Hell, I never knew there was any land in here open to settlement. Rosy and me, we happened to be riding along the south fence, back here, and we saw where some darn galoot had laid down the wires and drove a hull outfit through—from the looks of things. So consequently we fogged on over here—"

"I cannot tell a lie, Dilly. I did that myself. So would you, if you'd been in my place. It was almost dark and raining to beat four of a kind. I'd promised to show these boys the location of their claims, so I took a short cut. I meant to ride back in to Camas this morning and I thought I'd fix the fence on my way out. You don't seem to have any stock in here."

"No—No, that part's all right, Mr. King. We just didn't know it was you. And comin' on it like that, we was kinda on the peck, I s'pose. Then we couldn't get much satisfaction outa your friend here—"

Than looked up, squinting one eye that was fast purpling. "You sure tried hard enough, puncher."

"Yeah. I tried." Dilly remembered something. "Seen anything of Rosy, Mr. King? Darn chump, he was right here a minute ago, holding my coat."

"Here he comes." Blaney pointed to the grove. "Looks as though he got kinda excited and run off."

53

The small cowpuncher rode up, full of apologies. "Your damn horse broke loose," he said three separate times. Then Blaney gravely introduced him to Than.

Jerry Rose was the odd name he bore. With the exception of needing a shave, he much resembled a chubby boy of twelve. He listened solemnly to Blaney King, then pulled off his hat and leaned down to shake hands. Than nearly laughed aloud. Jerry Rose was almost completely bald. The fringe of hair around the base of his skull was curly and a bright sorrel lightly sprinkled with white. But the gray horse he bestrode looked a mean treacherous brute, only to be controlled through fear of his rider, and the gun on Rosy's hip had a holster scarred with long use. Than read these signs correctly and shook hands with no more smiling than was polite. Rosy, he decided, was not a man to be laughed at.

"That your brother, been coughing his head off in there?" Rosy jerked a thumb toward the tent. Than gave a surprised nod. He had forgotten Dade, had not even been conscious of that rending cough which seized Dade every morning lately.

"Lunger, ain't he?" Rosy queried further and he did not trouble to lower his voice. "That what brought yuh out here, hunh?"

There was abrupt movement within the tent. The loose tent flaps were flung violently aside and Dade came out, shaking with anger—or exhaustion; it was difficult to say which. He had a sixshooter in his hand, and with an identifying glance around the little group, he leveled the gun at Jerry Rose.

"You'll apologize for that remark or I'll feed you every bullet in this gun!" he stated with a deadly kind of calm.

CHAPTER SEVEN

THERE WAS ONE STUNNED MOMENT WHEN THE tableau held. It was Than who broke it. With an angry stride he reached Dade and wrenched the gun from his hand. "What the devil ails you, Dade! You crazy?"

His other hand went up, clutched Dade's shoulder and shook it as if he were trying to break a nightmare. "Seems to me you're getting pretty darn previous, flourishing a gun around like that."

Coughing, gripping the tent pole for support, Dade jerked himself free. "You mind your—g—damned business!" he gasped between coughs. "They're Tepee men—looking for trouble. They—they'll get a bellyful––" His voice was high and husky, tense with hysterical rage. To hear him coughing like that, gasping for breath to curse and threaten, was horrible.

"Oh, shut up! Don't be a fool," Than cut in sharply.

"You keep your nose—out of this! Called me a lunger! I'll damned quick show him—I'll kill the first—" A fresh paroxysm seized him and halted the mad words. He doubled forward, swaying against the pole so that the tent shook with a dull rattle of canvas.

Blaney stepped up, got him by the other arm, signaled Than with his eyes. "Fool trick, letting you ride all day in the rain before your case of grippe was over with," he said, with a steadying matter-of-factness. "Place for you is back in your blankets till that cold's busted. How about some hot coffee, Than?"

Than nodded, dropped Dade's arm and went for the coffee, handing it in through the tent doorway to Blaney, who gave him a queer, worried look before he dropped the flap and turned his attention to pacifying

Dade.

Than looked at the two Tepee riders, beckoning them over beyond the camp fire out of hearing from the tent. "My brother's got a touch of T.B. all right," he explained soberly, "and he's sensitive as the devil about it. Sorry, Mr. Rose. You'll just have to lay that little outbreak to fever—or nerves."

Dilly pulled down the corners of his mouth. "Hell, I wouldn't think there was anything much the matter with his nerve—or yours either. Locating in another man's field—that takes the nerve of a brass monkey."

"Talk about your brass monkeys! How about the nerve of a man throwing a fence around two or three sections of open land and trying to hog it in with his own?"

"Yeah—well, it ain't any skin off my nose," Dilly replied laconically and felt his hurts. "I'm willin' to let the boss do his own squabbling over that. Kinda looks to me like the law's on your side, anyway." He glanced toward Blaney, who was coming over from the tent. "How about it, Mr. King? All right and according to Hoyle, these fellows movin' in on us like this?"

"I'd hardly be here with them, prepared to help them locate their lines, if it weren't according to Hoyle," Blaney said shortly. "Than, that brother of yours is a sick man, if I'm any judge. How about it? Think we ought to haul him back to the doctor?"

Than considered for a moment. "Well, he wouldn't have a doctor in town when he was as bad as this, so I don't suppose he'd stand for it out here," he said finally. "Of course, if you think he's in any danger—"

Blaney shook his head. "Hell, I'm no doctor, Than. But I know fever when I see it."

"Yeah," Than told him dryly, "it's that slow fever of

56

his we're out here to try to cure. Dade's always on a hair trigger when he's feeling punk. At home, we don't pay any attention to him when he flies off the handle. Hope you didn't take it serious, Mr. Rose." He grinned suddenly at the childish figure on the mean gray horse.

"Oh, my, no!" Rosy assured him in a deceptively soft treble voice. "If I'd 'a' took him serious, you'd be pullin' a blanket up over his face long b'fore this. No, no; I seen by the way he handled his gun, 't he didn't know which end the bullet was comin' out of. Man can get all the killin' he wants, without takin' advantage of a pilgrim like him. 'N' Mr. King's friend too; no, I never took him serious at all."

"That's all right, then." Blaney stifled a laugh provoked by Dilly's lowered eyelid. "Say, is any good purpose served by letting this breakfast go to waste?"

Than listened toward the tent, heard nothing and moved to the fire. "No good purpose in the world, that I know of. You fellows better come have some breakfast; a cup of coffee, anyway."

The Tepee riders looked at each other. Now that breakfast was mentioned, the aroma of slowly bubbling coffee was tempting. Dilly heaved a great sigh.

"Course, we'd oughta start right in makin' you homesteaders hard to catch," he temporized with his duty. "And I'd oughta take another fall outa you for cuttin' my lip like you did on my one buck tooth. I always do hate to get into a fight, just on that account. Just as sure as hell, I get my lip slammed against that tooth. On the other hand—"

"I'll have a cup of coffee with yuh," Rosy accepted so promptly that Dilly couldn't finish. "We ain't had no orders yet about runnin' you outa here, and I'm always friendly as I kin be if I git half a chance."

"Here's a cup, then. Help yourself. Better have some of this bannock and bacon too. I can fry more in no time at all." Than filled a plate and proffered it to Rosy, who grinned and took it.

Dilly took an eager step forward. "I guess it's good etiquette to eat a bite with yuh," he said. "Rosy's plumb right; we ain't never had any orders about what to do in a case of this kind. Hobe Cheever—he's the foreman— he wouldn't make a move without orders from the old man, and Bearnson, he's in Helena and there's no tellin' when he'll be back." He took full plate and cup from Than and looked around for a place to sit down. "Hell, they don't pay us to read their minds," he added plaintively.

A glow of friendliness filled Than. These were men after his own heart; the kind he knew best. They were like Blaney, doing their work as well as they knew how, but reserving the right to be human. Even his fight with Dilly could not chill the warmth of their instinctive liking for each other nor leave a sting that went deeper than their bruises.

"Bearnson's sure going to be su'prised when he gits home and finds you folks settlin' in here," Rose observed reflectively, speaking around a generous bite of bannock and bacon.

"Surprised!" Dilly echoed and nearly choked on a swallow of very sweet coffee. "Gosh!"

Than eyed the two. "We're not exactly looking for the glad hand," he volunteered, grinning a little. "At the same time, we're here to stay. This land was vacant and we filed on it. It isn't our fault if your boss ran a fence around it. That's illegal and he knows it."

"Yeah, you've got the law on your side, all right. Boss'll be back before very long, I reckon. He wouldn't

58

miss being here when round-up starts."

"Hobe'll be throwin' the saddle bunch in this field next week," Rosy spoke up, rolling his childish blue eyes toward the horses. "You wanta watch out yourn don't mix with 'em."

"Well, thanks for the tip. Looks like we'll be stringing wire, about the first thing we do." Than was studying Dilly's profile as he spoke, and at that moment Dilly looked up and met his gaze with a keen inquiring glance.

"Say," Than asked him curiously, "weren't you working over on the Musselshell, about three years ago? You and Pipe Morgan—"

"Gosh, yes! Pipe and me was over there riding for the Two Box, gathering up the tail end of them Oxbow cattle the Two Box bought and couldn't shove off the Musselshell the fall before, on account of that big storm—" Dilly slapped a free hand down on one knee. "I got it! I thought you looked awful familiar, back there when we was gettin' our second wind and watchin' for a new handhold. I knew darned well I'd saw you before. I got yuh placed, now. You're the jasper that swum the Musselshell on a bet and your horse rolled over with yuh in midstream. Pipe, he rode into swimmin' water, swingin' his loop to nail yuh, but you went on downstream and grabbed a willow branch as you was sailin' around the bend." Dilly shook his head in pleased incredulity and added, "Well, I'll be damned!"

"I thought your name was Brandt," Than explained. "That's what fooled me. And you're thinner. Brandt. That's what they called you, all right."

"Yeah, old Pipe started callin' me Brandt. Up here they've kinda swapped ends on my name and call me Dilly. And you was Kid Roberts, as I recollect it. I never

59

heard yuh called anything but that. Kid Roberts. I remember—"

"Kid Roberts!" Rosy exploded, leaning their way. "This the Kid Roberts that used to work for the Diamond S, over there? Why, say! I've heard the boys tell about you, time and again. Quite a bronc rider, from all I used to hear. You know Billy Bevins?"

"Billy? Sure I do! So does Blaney, here. Blaney wasn't with me that spring Brandt—or Dilly, rather—speaks of, but he was back riding in the fall. Sugarfoot. Maybe you boys heard about him."

Evidently they had and had also heard why Blaney was called Sugarfoot over on the Musselshell three years before. Dilly repeated that he would be damned, laughing when he said it. Rosy whooped with glee and told the story as he had heard it; which had best not be repeated here.

There was no more talk of homesteads or of illegal ways of hogging open land for winter range. The sun swung high while the three squatted there, gossiping of men and horses they knew.

There was much laughter, some pungent criticisms and a good deal of picturesque profanity. Cigarette stubs littered the outer edge of cooling ashes while the fire died to whitened embers. The Tepee horses stood half asleep and switched at early flies, and the eight around the wagon dozed patiently with empty nosebags on, waiting until some one came back out of the past and remembered that there was much to be done that day and for many days thereafter.

It was Dade who broke the spell at last. Twice he had parted the tent flaps and looked out, scowling at the four sitting there on the ground, smoking and talking as if they never would stop. Now he came stalking out to the group, eyes blazing with anger and the fever that smoldered in his veins.

"Sorry to interrupt the love feast," he told them, "but I was under the impression that we came here to stake out our claims and get started to building. If it's a cowboy conference, I'll have to ask you fellows to sit somewhere else so that I can cook myself something to eat. I, at least, have work to do."

Rosy was telling exactly where and how and why a certain "glass-eye" bronc had learned that it was exceedingly unwise to take liberties with one Gerald Rose. He was slowly and painstakingly working up to the dramatic climax and he hated interruptions, anyway. He moved one chubby leg away from Dade's encroaching foot, got to his feet and drew himself up to his full stature (which was exactly four feet and eleven inches). He cast a baleful look up at Dade, opened his mouth to speak, closed it tightly and turned his back in silent scorn. With a surprising agility he mounted the Roman-nosed gray and rode off, without a word. Dilly followed him.

Than wheeled angrily upon Dade. "Just because you're under the weather doesn't give you any license to be so damned insulting," he cried.

Dade's mouth twisted in the smile he could make so exasperating. "You can't insult a cowboy," he retorted. "Furthermore, I don't believe in hobnobbing with the enemy."

Than turned from watching the riders go galloping out of sight over the slope's uneven crest. His eyes and mouth looked bitter, with a loneliness beneath the hurt.

"If those boys are enemies of ours," he said, "you'll be the cause of it. Remember that."

CHAPTER EIGHT

BLANEY WAS FURIOUS; BUT HE REMINDED HIMSELF THAT it wasn't his put-in unless Dade spat some of his venom in his direction; so he clamped his teeth against the things he wanted to say and walked away to the wagon. As he took the nosebags off the horses and led them in pairs to the creek for a drink, he wondered just how much abuse Than thought he was supposed to endure before he fought back. Sick or well, that young hound needed to have the tar knocked out of him a time or two, he thought with rare vindictiveness.

Than stolidly fried bacon and bannock for Dade's breakfast and reheated the coffee to the tune of Dade's biting sarcasm. He was used to these senseless tirades and he knew much of that ill temper came of having been forgotten—overlooked for a time. The thing Dade hated most was to have his vituperations ignored, yet the answer soft enough to turn away his wrath had still to be found. So Than finished his cooking and proceeded to wash the dishes with a detached air of complete boredom and then went over to where Blaney was saddling his horse.

"You going to ride?" he asked, with some surprise, because he had always supposed that land lines were paced off afoot.

Blaney stooped to reach the dangling cinch under the belly of his big roan that turned its head to watch him with wise eyes.

"We'll have to or that bull-headed brother of yours will try to walk too. Moreover, there's considerable ground to cover."

"Oh. I see." Than saddled the easy-gaited little sorrel

he had bought for Dade, led it out away from the wagon and dropped its rein ends to the ground, then picked up his own saddle and carried it to where Black Hawk stood. With a jerk of his head, he called Blaney over to him.

"Wish you'd run Dade's lines first," he muttered. "And don't pay any attention to his grouchiness. He'll come out of it. He always tries to get a rise out of somebody when he's feeling rocky. I want to put up his shack first, on his homestead see?"

"I get you." From the tail of his eye, he saw Dade approaching. "Better bring along a hatchet and any rags you've got handy, for flags. There's plenty of willows all down along the creek."

Than nodded, rummaged in the wagon and got what was needed. Without another word they mounted and set off down the creek, Dade riding moodily behind the two, his shoulders dropped forward, his thin body slack in the saddle.

Blaney made a sweeping gesture with one hand. "Your mother's homestead. If I'm not mistaken, we're riding across the upper end of it now. Her claim lies between the two of you. I had an idea that's the way you boys would like to have it, when I filled in the descriptions."

"That's fine and dandy," Than agreed.

Dade said nothing at all, but his eyes lifted to gaze about him with the first real interest he had shown in the country. Whether he was disappointed or pleased, no one could guess.

"I thought we'd ride on down to Dade's east line, locate that and work back up," Blaney went on. "I think I know about where it is but we may have to hunt around a little. You see that clump of cottonwoods off there? If I'm any judge of distance, Dade's homestead should just about take in that grove. All this along here is fine hayland."

"Here's where I'll put up my cabin," Dade announced in his ordinary tone, which was quite pleasant and which rather startled Blaney. "I'll fence this whole flat, here, both sides of the creek. That ought to take in ten acres, at least."

"Ought to fence the whole section, by rights," Than observed thoughtfully. "We can't do that now, but it seems to me all our bottomland should be fenced right away. If the Tepee throws a bunch of horses in here, this creek bottom is going to be fed down short before the grass gets a good start. And we'll have to figure on putting up all the hay we can cut this summer. I thought we'd maybe hire a couple of men for a month or two. There's *so darned* much to do before snow flies!"

How true a prophecy that was the following months revealed beyond all doubt. Where they had halted to gaze and plan, within ten days Dade's little twelve-by-sixteen claim shack stood backed against the grove and the fierce storms of winter, its two windows looking out upon rolling grassland; one giving a wide view of the lush meadowland and the other facing up the creek where his mother and Than would build.

As Than afterwards looked back upon them, those first months of homesteading seemed the busiest, yet the most tranquil months he had ever known. He remembered his amazement over Dade; how quickly he had gained strength and a certain acrid self-sufficiency that would not tolerate advice or interference; how eagerly he took possession of his cabin, hanging blankets over the gaping windows and doorway to shut out a chilling wind; and how the tap-tap of his hammer had sounded late into those first nights, as he worked away by lamplight, building shelves for his books, cupboards for food and dishes, a wardrobe for his clothes.

Than discovered traits in Dade he had never suspected, an aptitude for carpentry among them. He had always known Dade was self-centered, but here his natural selfishness found new ways of expression—as when he stayed at his shack, fussily beveling the edges of his shelf boards while Than grappled alone with the problem of getting Mom's shack covered with tar paper and battened down smoothly against the stiff breeze that seemed never to stop. At the time Than had mentally cursed Dade for a loafer; later, he vaguely suspected Dade of pottering with those shelves deliberately, wanting to hide the fact that heavier tasks were beyond his strength. Maybe not. Than never could be certain; but the suspicion had made him gentler, more patient.

Recalling those first months, Than always remembered the secret chagrin and the sense of anticlimax they had felt over Bearnson. Even the Tepee riders had expected. Bearnson to put up a fight. Bearnson had fooled them all. Mom had come down filled with the determination to defend her land with bullet or buckshot, if necessary Daily she had warned Than and Dade to look out for tricks such as fences cut in the night, ambushes out in the hills, horses stolen from the pasture—all the petty depredations commonly to be expected in a range feud. S. P. Bearnson was old Pete Bearnson of Helena and none other, she declared, even though she was forced to identify him by description alone. Being old Pete Bearnson, they could look out for any skullduggery a body could name.

Than always grinned when he thought of Mom that

first year and how she seemed actually disappointed that nothing happened. While Mom waited, grimly prepared to carry on a modified Indian warfare, Bearnson—who might or might not be old Pete of Helena—silently accepted the situation. True, he put up No Trespassing signs on that short cut across his field and made the nesters take the long way around his fence, but that was his legal right. Even Mom could not advise a shotgun argument over that.

"You watch out," she used to warn Than. "It ain't like old Pete to let go of anything he once gets his clutches on. We've come in here and took away a whole section of good land right from under his nose. He ain't goin' to give it up without a struggle—you mark my words!"

But there they were, ploughing and planting, fencing and building, working like beavers getting ready for a hard winter, and not a hand was raised against them. Bearnson was not an amiable man or a friendly one. His life seemed to center on building up his herds and his bank account. Friendships were luxuries in which he had no time to indulge. He went his way, nodded when he met his neighbors in the trail, spoke to his men only when he had an order to give, and his conferences with Hobe Cheever, his foreman, were never long and apparently concerned only the business of running his ranch.

If he objected to the Roberts family settling in the choicest end of his big field, fencing his cattle from a mile of the creek and the wooded shelter it offered, turning acres of rich upland ruthlessly into great black squares of cultivated land, he did not mention the fact. So far as Than could see, Bearnson accepted their presence just as he would have accepted a storm which raised his percentage of loss through the winter. They

66

were there; they had a legal right to be there. Bearnson ignored their presence.

With the cowboys it was different. Looking back, Than could see that Dade never was accepted by the Tepee riders; from Hobe Cheever, Dilly and Rose, to Syd Hunt and Dod (whose name was Jim Dodson) the outfit stood on guard with Dade. They seemed to think he was like a tricky horse, never to be trusted. After that first morning's encounter they made no overtures toward friendship. They were afraid of his sarcasm, resentful of his superior manner. They endured Dade for the sake of Than and Mom and Susan; any one could see that.

Great months, those. Hungry riders galloping down the slope to the gate in the new wire fence—a civilized, nicely balanced gate of one-by-six bars well braced; a gate easily managed from the saddle and never left open—as it might have been had the Tepee boys been less friendly. Lean young fellows racing the rest of the way as they were wont to race into round-up camp at mealtime.

They "swiped" Susan's hair ribbons to tie upon their bridles, flaunting each new treasure before the rest. They sniffed eagerly the appetizing odors that came from Mom's kitchen on baking days and thought themselves ill-used if they must ride off without sampling her doughnuts or pies. They sat through long winter evenings playing cards around her extension table in the kitchen, and ate hot buttered popcorn which they scooped up with a saucer when the heaped dishpan was passed around the table between games. Being a good Methodist, Mom had never approved of cards. It had taken Dilly, the persuasive one, two whole evenings to bring Mom to the point of recklessly adjusting her

67

spectacles so that she could see the cards held gingerly in her blue-veined hands.

Her mouth had puckered at her own wickedness. "My land, I don't know what the Ladies Aid would think of me if they could see me this minute," she sighed whimsically—though her eyes twinkled through her glasses when she looked up at Dilly leaning over her chair. "But if I'm goin' to break you boys of card-playing, I want to know what there is about it to take up your minds. Which one is high-low Jack? This smirkly one? Jackanapes, I'd call him (Baby, take my knittin' away from that pesky cat and put her outside!) Is it my turn now? What sh'll I do?"

As Than remembered it, Mom had speedily learned what she should do. She learned so thoroughly that she became a terror to the unwary. "It's for all the world like fightin' Injuns," she said once, clicking her teeth triumphantly while she remorselessly swept in the trick that won a hard-fought game. "You got to study out what they're goin' t' do, and then beat 'em to it."

Not always did they play cards, however. Than always smiled as he recalled one stiff, uncomfortable evening when Susan played Beethoven and Bach and Chopin on the new upright piano he had hauled in for her birthday, that first fall. The Tepee boys left early, that evening, and Susan had been a little hurt. But when Than told her why, she saw the point, all right. The next time they came she sang "Bonnie Black Bess" and started them off on all the old songs they knew. Since Mom put her foot down on Sunday card-playing, it was then they sang themselves hoarse.

There were other times when they blew out the lamp and sat in the flickering light of the cottonwood logs blazing in Mom's cherished fireplace. Sitting cross-legged on the floor or sprawled propped on elbows, the Tepee boys told tales of the round-up, of bad horses and bad men and bad storms, while the wind whined over the chimney and the snow built a tiny drift under the door—or so Than always pictured it.

Poignant memories, these. Unforgettable pictures in which the Tepee cowboys always stood out clean-cut and friendly. He could see them stamping feet into their "artics," fingers groping for the buckles, even the smell of warm rubber after the overshoes had lain in a pile close to the warm hearth. He saw them lingering to button sour dough or big fur coats to their smooth-shaven chins which sometimes showed the pinkish cut of a razor plied too hurriedly. Then the squeak of frosty snow and the yellow lantern light on the shovel-marked drifts as he led the way to the stable where the saddled horses stood two in a stall, eyeballs shining as they looked out from the shadows.

The Tepee cowboys were not the only ones who rode that way, found the social oasis in that bleak wind-swept land and came again. Frank Hoskins was one.

Frank was holding down a homestead (whispered gossip said Bearnson was to be his buyer when the land was patented) over in Snowbird Coulee, which opened to Running Man Creek just below the Tepee's east line fence. He had a desert claim back up on the bench, and during the roundup season he usually rode for the Tepee outfit and so was considered almost one of the outfit. It is possible that gossip concerning the ultimate ownership of his claims came to his ears or Bearnson's and made a change advisable, because Frank had found a new boss, about the time when the Roberts family moved to the Broken Hills country. All that spring and later in the fall, Frank had worked for Sandy

69

MacHardie, a long-lipped old Scot whose cattle mingled with the Tepee herds on the open range, and whose home ranch lay ten miles farther down Running Man Creek. MacHardie was as strict a Presbyterian as Mom was Methodist, and predestination never could tolerate Mom's creed of falling from grace and sinning seventy times seven, with a good prospect of salvation at last through an eleventh-hour repentance. There was no ground there for friendly intercourse and the families would probably have remained apart but for Jean.

Jean was tall, slim, blue-eyed and with black hair that lay in thick waves upon her head. She rode like a cowboy, could swing a rope and know where its loop would drop, could shoot at least three of the pips from a five-spot card—at a fairly close range, if you must have the exact truth—and her laugh had in it somewhere a suggestion of harp strings plucked softly. She had a way of using her father's accent with devastating effect, though when she forgot her "Scotch" and spoke plain American, she had best be taken seriously because she was then in no mood for trifling.

Frank Hoskins brought her over one Sunday evening with the Tepee boys, because he had promised to bring his violin and play with Susan, and there was a twitter and a chattering when the two girls met. The same school and the same classes in Great Falls—no more than that was needed for the building of an intimate friendship.

If Than failed to include Jean MacHardie in his pleasant memories of that year's neighborings with the Tepee outfit, it was only because she had a special and extremely important place of her own.

But always there was Frank Hoskins, dark, silent, keen-eyed and watchful, obtruding his saturnine presence in any picture that held Jean. So all the memories were not pleasant and life for Than during those first two years had its complexities after all.

CHAPTER NINE

ON A FINE DAY IN MID-SEPTEMBER, JEAN MACHARDIE rode up across the Tepee field on Running Man, following the creek regardless of trails, which was a way she had of doing when she rode for pleasure and had no one with her. Sometimes she rode at top speed, as if she would outrun the thoughts that shadowed her eyes, and again she would pull her horse down to a walk and go loitering along with bridle reins drooping and her eyes veiled in reverie; a strange mood for Jean MacHardie, whose sane, humorous outlook on life seemed undaunted by anything that might come to her.

At the wire gate giving access to Dade Roberts' homestead she swung off, supple as a boy, lifted the wire loop off the stake and dragged the gate out of the way of her shiny sorrel as it went mincing through. With some effort she replaced the gate as she had found it, making sure that the loop of twisted baling wire was pushed well down over the stake. Not many cattle and horses were in the Tepee field, but things were going along so smoothly between cattleman and nesters that it would be a pity for trespassing stock to disturb the peace.

Just within the fence stood Dade's cornfield, the scanty crop already cut and shocked. It looked to Jean as if Dade had slyly dared the Tepee outfit to turn their cattle in and see what would happen. But range cattle know nothing of corn and the fence remained intact.

71

The patch stood like a shaggy village of very small Indian wigwams, deserted by all save scattered flocks of crows and blackbirds, fattening in unaccustomed ease. There wouldn't be enough corn left to feed the few hogs Dade persisted in raising, even after the Roberts family carried a cattle brand of its own, with a couple of hundred mixed yearlings to start their herd. Dade had planted lavishly enough—there must be ten or fifteen acres of corn—but he had not taken care of it afterwards. The field was overgrown with weeds; tall wild sunflowers nodding their late blossoms on half-dried stalks, mustard, thistles scattering seed for next year.

Jean preferred the unscarred prairie. She was glad to be out of the field, through another wire gate and into Dade's meadow. Here was the sweet tangy odor of ripe stubble and new hay. Three long stacks stood within their wire enclosure. Jean gave a quick involuntary frown as she rode past. It wasn't her business and she certainly did not mean to give advice to Dade Roberts, but if he had any sense at all he'd plough a good wide fire-break around that hay corral. Well, if she saw him, perhaps she might mention it.

Dade was not at home. His neat, bare cabin wore an empty look and on this balmy day the windows were closed. As she rode through the yard, taking the hard-packed trail up the creek across Mom Roberts' homestead, Jean thought how like himself Dade had made his place. Perfectly clean yard, stable and corral looking almost unused, they were so orderly, but no friendly welcoming look. A place where people were not expected to come except on business; almost like an office, Jean thought, and smiled at the thought. Then she sent her sorrel galloping up the trail with an impulse to leave Dade's homestead behind her. A sour, selfish young man she had found him; not here because he loved the open country, but here to make money; sneering at the people he met, turning up his nose at the hardships, thinking always of the town and of himself as an exile. Five years of exile—Jean had heard him say it. After that, he said, the folks would have to shift for themselves. He certainly didn't intend to live like a hermit all his life. A fine spirit, that!

Half a mile up the creek stood Mom's roomy log cabin with its rock fireplace and its flower garden— nipped with frost, but still showing a few sturdy blossoms. Mom's place seemed to hold out its arms and smile; like Mom Roberts herself, Jean thought, with a warm light in her eyes.

Here too was thrift, but hominess and a snug look of comfort went with it. There were long haystacks also, plus two squatty stacks of wheat for Mom's chickens. Yellow pumpkins lay in a denuded corn patch, and fat green squashes were dark blobs among their wilted vines in the garden. Long rows of autumn-leaved carrots and parsnips with never a weed to spoil the clean lines. Beets, cabbages, turnips—Jean rode slowly past, thinking of the times she had found Mom there, grimly plying her hoe. Chickens wandered everywhere, and up from the creek waddled a flock of white ducks, quacking sociably as they came. Over by the stacks were turkeys, and out in the grain stubble six gray geese walked with stately stride, snatching grasshoppers between their patient gleaning of wheat grains. Mom Roberts certainly knew how to make a home in the wilderness.

Within call, yet well across the dividing fence that marked the boundary line of Mom's homestead, Than's

73

cabin stood frankly bare of all save the essential things required of homesteaders. Than slept there, according to the law that said he must. He had his own cultivated land, his own haystacks, his own stable and corral. But the log cabin was home, nevertheless. Any one who rode that way would know that Than Roberts had built his cabin where he could keep a protective eye upon his womenfolk—and they would also understand that he was giving no man an excuse for contesting his claim on the ground that he was not complying with the law.

Jean gave Than's cabin a long, interested glance as she dismounted at Mom's gate. Of course he wouldn't be there in the middle of the day. She was so preoccupied with wondering where he was that she had reached Mom's door and had knocked before it occurred to her that the place was strangely silent. Never had she ridden over for a visit and found Susan and her mother away from home; there were so few places to go. But now, when she tried the door, she found it locked. She stood on the doorstep and gazed disconsolately around, her eyes straying toward Than's shack much oftener than she realized and with a wistfulness she would have died rather than reveal in words. But after a minute or two she remounted her horse and rode away, following the grass ribboned trail across Than's homestead to the gate next the hills, where the dim trail of the two homesteaders over to the west (Gus Dahlburg and Fred Lamar were their names) joined the Roberts road in its circuitous route to the highway.

Jean let herself through the gate and, leaving the road, she took to the hills. But after all she did not ride far; only to the top of the first ridge, where the view down the valley and away past her father's ranch gave ample reason for halting. Where a granite ledge jutted out from the hillside she dismounted and sat on a flat brown rock, letting her horse nibble grass as far as his long bridle reins would permit. When he pulled harder, wanting a particularly tempting morsel just beyond his reach, the reins slid from her loose clasp and the horse grazed at ease, dragging the reins after him as he fed.

Jean scarcely noticed. She was staring thoughtfully down upon the valley and the Roberts ranch, and she was thinking of the changed outlook since last she perched here. Two years ago, that must have been; and all that land was wild pasture, with no fences save the one enclosing Bearnson's big pasture along the creek. Why, she had not dreamed then that she'd be worrying–

—

"Small credit to me that I'd be thinking twice about a man that hasn't a glance for me," she finished the thought aloud. "He's a tongue in his head, if there's anything he would say to me, and I'll mind my pride and keep my thoughts at home. And myself with them," she added, with a glum humor.

But she made no immediate move to take her thoughts and her pride and ride home with them. She had that instant seen a horseman riding into a gully half a mile away and her eyes glued their gaze to the place where he must presently ride out into sight again.

"If I'd the sense of a hen turkey, I'd ride away home," she told herself bitterly, when she had looked until her eyes watered. But she didn't go home. She watched that gully, thinking that the rider would surely appear any moment now. He must, if he followed the road in either direction, because it crossed the gully just outside the Tepee fence. He couldn't ride on through the fence. He would show himself, since he must be taking a short cut to the road, and she wanted very much to know who he was; because even a girl who is minding her pride and taking her thoughts and herself home might reach the Roberts gate in time to have it opened by a young man coming down the road to the same point. That is, she might, if he were riding a high-stepping black horse named Hawk.

How long she sat there watching, Jean could not tell. She was recalled to her surroundings when her sorrel horse, Robin, gave a great snort and went tearing down the slope, tail up and head turned sidewise, so that the dangling reins would not trip and throw him as he galloped. Angling away from him toward the wooded hills behind, a gray wolf ran like a leaping shadow against the brown of the grass.

Jean leaped to her feet and shouted. "Robin! Whoa! Stop it, ye fool! Canna' ye see it's only a wolf?" A girl less accustomed to horses would have run after him; Jean stood where she was and called him names while she watched the route he took. He'd be going home, of course, but with the gates all closed he would be some time getting there. He would have to follow the Tepee fence around; a good eight miles, none of them smooth traveling.

"An' the best I could wish for ye is that the reins break the neck o' ye," was her final word, as she turned and looked across the ridge she was on. What or who could have scared that wolf into streaking it for the hills? He ran as if he had been shot at, but that couldn't be. She would have heard a gunshot, with the wind blowing down from the hills.

She walked over to where she could look down into the next little coulee. It wasn't more than a few rods. On the edge of the steep slope she stopped and stared.

76

Directly below her, thin blue ribbons of smoke drifted together from various points in the grassfilled hollow. Even as she stood there, a gust of wind swooped down, caught the smoke and sent it billowing upward, bearing to her nostrils the unmistakable tangy odor of burning grass; and gazing deeper, past the smoke, she saw a jagged, leaping red line of flame. Another lift of the smoke showed her a narrow strip of blackened ground where the fire had already passed. It must have burned slowly just at first, until it reached out from the tangle of berry bushes in there and began eating the heavy grass.

Not so very fast was it burning, nor did the flames rise very high. Until that line of fire left the hollow there was no harm that it could do. But once outside— Involuntarily Jean turned her head toward the Roberts ranch and to the long stacks of hay. Suddenly she recalled something she had not consciously noticed as she rode past these upper stacks. Dade was not the only careless one of the lot; even Than had not yet burned a fireguard around his place.

"And this is the time I must be set afoot!" Jean exclaimed between her teeth, and started running down the steep slope, directly toward the nearest line of fire. "And my bare hands to fight it!" she added, voicing the culmination of her dismay.

But as she reached the grassy level and met the heat and the acrid smoke gases full in her face, her hands dropped to her waist, swift fingers busy. Then with a twist and a shake of her slender body she stooped, caught her falling skirt and stepped out of it. Holding the ankle-length divided skirt by the band and using it as a club, she squinted her eyes against the smoke and went to work.

It was vigorous exercise for a girl, but Jean

MacHardie had been born on a ranch and she knew a great deal about prairie fires. With a clocklike regularity her arms rose and fell, beating down the licking flames as she walked slowly forward, leaving a charred black line of burnt grass smoking behind her.

Within five minutes her arms ached frightfully, but each one of those minutes brought the blaze nearer to the open prairie. She dared not stop to rest, even to wipe a cinder from her eye. Too much depended upon the next few minutes. Once she glanced aside toward a small grass-filled gully, wondering if it held water enough to wet the heavy cloth of her skirt. Already it was black, breaking into scorched tatters. No matter— she could not stop to look for water. Probably there wouldn't be any; it had been a dry fall, she remembered, as she fought her way along the line, beating, beating— a never-ending, nightmare task.

Once she spoke aloud: "Twenty men cannot stop it, once it gets into the open!" And that thought drove her forward.

Time was not measured by moments; rather by endurance. She had thought this hollow in the hills too insignificant to be called a coulee, yet the distance across it seemed endless. She would not take time to straighten from her task, to look around her and see how far she had come or how much yet remained to do. Yet she was aware of the forward push, the new impetus to the flames. A subdued roar now rose and mingled with the snap and crackle that had filled her ears from the first. She knew what it meant, but she did not stop to look. She only swung harder, faster.

Then she was fighting out in the open and the cooler air of late afternoon was rushing in to fill the vortex formed by the heat. Before that gale the fire went leaping. And now, beyond the devouring rush of flame, a man in his shirt sleeves was flailing steadily with his coat. Through the smoke Jean saw him dimly and bent again to her work, her only reaction a fierce resentment because he had not come sooner.

Thud, thud, thud. They fought their way closer and closer together, the fire straining out ahead like ravening dogs on leash. On a gravelly slope where the grass was scanty, the two seemed likely to meet, but a gust of wind tore the foremost flames upward, lifted them across the last barren strip and flung them bodily into heavier grass growing matted with weeds along a shallow draw. The stubborn crackle became a triumphant roar. Sparks and black flakes of ash and burning leaves swept far out ahead. Like wild things turned loose, the small blazes were scattered before the wind, starting fresh fires as they raced ahead. Smoke billowed upward in a great rolling cloud. As if glorying in its hard-won freedom, great flames shot upward, leaped to fresh fuel of bush or weed and tore onward, borne by the rising wind.

CHAPTER TEN

ACROSS AN ACRID SPACE OF BLACKENED ASH, THAN and Jean stared at each other with smarting bloodshot eyes.

"And where were you keeping yourself all this while, I'd like to know?" Jean fiercely demanded. "You could have stopped it before it reached the open. Now, look!" One tired arm lifted wearily to point.

"We'll catch it when it hits that 'doby hollow this side the fence. Come on!" Than cried. "You go around

79

there and head off the south end. I'll take the north. Hurry up, before it gets into the heavy grass beyond!"

Jean's red-rimmed watery eyes felt the sting of real tears. "Man, do you think I'm a machine, then?"

But Than was already running to overtake the roaring wall of flame where it must halt and go nibbling through the scanty grass at the edge of the barren adobe. With a gasp of futile anger, Jean ran stumbling over the burnt stubble that scorched her feet even through the thick soles of her riding boots.

Another nightmare of fighting flames with a skirt charred to cinders halfway up its length. If only she could dip it in water, half the labor would be saved. One blow of a wet gunnysack, she told herself, would have equaled three of these. And the wind, sucked in to fill the vacuum created as the hot air roared upward, came whooping down from the hills and swept the flames onward.

Than was right. The adobe patch did check the fire, but only for a minute or two. Just when the two dared hope once more that they had got it under control, a great gust of wind lifted whole tufts of burning grass and carried them across to the richer sod beyond the adobe. New fires sprang up in a dozen places. These merged. A fresh wave of orange flame drove down upon the road, leaped it and went ravening across Than's pasture. Above it and before, a great brown cloud filled with sparks, ash flakes yet hot enough to kindle a new blaze, rolled and tumbled.

Than gave one long look, dropped the smoking rags that had been his coat, whirled and sprinted back across the burned ground, toward the hills. As he came thundering back down over the uneven slope on Hawk, Jean stumbled over to the gate, tugged loose the hot chain, swung the gate away from its blackened post.

Than pulled up, shouted at her as if she were far away. "Where's your horse? Get it and come on!"

"He ran off—"

"Climb on!" His left foot jerked from the stirrup. He reached out a hand.

Jean went up while Black Hawk gathered himself for a leap ahead. They were off, riding at right angles to the fire line, racing to pass its left flank before it could burn to the creek.

"Have to try and backfire!" Than shouted over his shoulder, as they went. "No fireguards—like a fool I kept putting it off from one day to the next—"

Jean had nothing to say. They wouldn't have time to backfire; not against that wind, and with the fire line growing yards wider every second. But perhaps they could save the house. That they were deliberately rushing to place themselves in front of that huge rolling wave of flame concerned her not at all. They had to fight it and if they could fight best out front—

But Than gave it thought, studying the battlefield as he spurred Hawk through the narrowing gap between fire and the grove of timber along the creek. He twisted half around within the embrace of her arms, his face turning until she could see his smoke-grimed cheek, the tight corner of his mouth.

"When we stop, you slide into the saddle and beat it across the creek," he directed tersely.

"I wull not!" Involuntarily her arms tightened their clasp.

"You've got to. You—you'll have to ride and warn the neighbors."

"If they're not warned by the smoke, small heed wull they give to onything I could say," Jean replied with

81

disconcerting logic. "Your shirt has a great hole burned in the back of it," she added, as if that somehow clinched her argument.

Than said no more but that did not mean he was yielding the point. As he reined Hawk directly into the path of the fire sweeping down upon them no more than a quarter of a mile away, his eyes kept darting quick glances this way and that, weighing chances.

At the hay corral he pulled up, threw his right leg over Hawk's neck and jumped. His feet had no more than struck the ground when Jean landed lightly behind him. Than whirled fiercely upon her, his eyes stern with anxiety.

"Pile on and drift! Good God, don't you know there's just one chance in a thousand? I can't let you take the risk, Jean." He handed her the reins.

Jean gave him one look, then turned and swung up into the saddle. "Start your fires well out, laddie, and be quick!" she cried, and was off and away.

With an unaccountable sinking of heart, Than rushed straight out toward the fire, across the uneven black ridge of three ploughed furrows, a strip of unmown weedy grass, to a second ploughed line. Just beyond this he knelt beside a thick tuft of grass, flicked his thumbnail across a match head, cupped the tiny blaze within his two palms, nursed the growing flame gently in under a matted nest of fine grasses. Still on one knee, he swept out his hands, pulling grass in handfuls, twisting it into a clumsy torch while he watched his new little fire fight for its life as a fierce hot gust whipped it to earth. One moment he feared it was out; the next that whole tuft suddenly ignited with a spatter of sparks. It spread to the next tuft, started to eat stealthily backward into the teeth of the wind.

Than waited no longer. Thrusting his twisted grass into the flames, he ran stooping, dragging his blazing torch across the grass close against the outer furrow. Where he ran, behind him a new small line of fire sprang into life. If he could carry that line far enough, if it could eat far enough back away from the furrows, and did not jump them and run toward the stacks and the buildings, that surge of flame rolling in across the pasture might yet be checked.

But the wind was now blowing a gale, driving the smoke down upon him. Already his first fire he had set could scarcely be seen in the acrid brown cloud. But when he looked out to the west, there beneath the roar and crackle, the smother of sparks and smoke, he saw the leaping line of flame. His backfire looked puny, yet it was developing a small roar of its own, and in two or three places it had jumped the slight barrier of ploughed ground and was halfway across to the inner furrows.

With the shock of a blow he remembered something. He had dropped his coat back there where the fire got out of control. Now he had nothing except his hat to beat out the flames running toward the stacks. Because the day promised to be warm, he had left off his chaps when he saddled Hawk right after dinner. He wished he had those heavy dogskin chaps now, he thought, as he snatched off his hat and started back.

"Come get the sacks and wet them, laddie, quick!" Jean called hoarsely, out there in the brown murk. "And you could carry one of the buckets, if ye wull!"

"Good glory! Jean! What the devil are you doing back here?" In long leaps Than was beside her, sloshing precious water as he snatched the bucket from her hands. He grabbed two grain sacks from off her shoulders, paused long enough to souse them in the bucket and started running. "Why didn't you do as you were told?" he shouted fiercely as he ran.

Jean kept pace with him. "You'd be in a sorry plight if I had," she told him, unabashed. "Give me a sack and stop your blithering. You'll need all your breath for the work before ye, I'm thinking."

"No! Go back! Get on Hawk and beat it, I tell you!"

"I wull not!"

"Mule!" gritted Than, and felt a wet sack slipping from his grasp, just as he reached the first line of ploughing. Even this line his backfire had jumped, running before the wind. Like a madman he fell to work, beating the flames down, every blow of the wet sack quenching the fire it fell upon. A little beyond him, he could hear the thud, thud of Jean's sack keeping pace with him, blow for blow.

A brave fight, but a losing one. A fiery hail of sparks fell around them. The hot wind seared their lungs, smoke blinded them. And still Than fought stubbornly, knowing he had lost.

Jean caught him by the arm, pulled him back. Her voice was shrill, tragically insistent. "The stacks are on fire! Come away to the hoose, laddie!"

Than gave one look, saw that she was right. He caught her wrist, gripped it and ran, pulling her along.

"All hell—can't stop it—now," he panted, glancing over his shoulder. "Where's—Hawk?"

"Tied to the gate!" gasped Jean, and felt him let go her wrist. "Where—?"

"Babe's pony—in the corral. Go on! I'll open—"

"Ye wull not!" Running, Jean caught his hand, held him back. "I'll do it. Do you get what papers— valuables—from the hoose! I'll come."

She was right. There was time enough, if she hurried.

84

But Than would not let her go alone. When it came to the point, he couldn't. They swerved aside and together they worked furiously. Than picked up a rope, jerked open the corral gate, ran and caught Susan's pony, leading him out, saddled him in record time. Jean in the stable was already boosting a calf out through the door. Chickens were cackling, leaning forward, necks outstretched as they ran. Waddling ducks quacked, tried to fly with their stunted wings, finished by squattering along on their webbed feet, wings flailing crookedly against the wind and smoke. The six gray geese had left the stubble long ago and were somewhere down the creek, swimming for dear life, their loud raucous honking plainly to be heard above the roaring crackle of the fire.

"Get on this horse now and beat it!" Than said harshly and laid the reins of the frightened pony in Jean's hands. He raced to his cabin, pulled on his chaps, another coat, rifled his homemade desk of papers and what money he had. No time for more. Already the three haystacks were a furnace and the pole corral was burning. Fire was licking along the logs of the stable up to the pole-and-dirt roof. He ran to Mom's cabin, burst in the door without waiting to get the key hidden under a flowerpot on the porch. Jean, holding the two horses quiet at the gate, watched him go.

"Be quick in there," she entreated him. "The fire's at your cabin, Than!"

The horses were snorting, eyes staring in terror. A girl less superbly sure of herself in the saddle could never have managed the two. Jean coaxed them, scolded, threatened—held them with her voice and her tired hands firm on the reins. The minutes seemed hours.

Than came running out oddly burdened; a Maltese cat

85

yowling under one arm, a brown cloth bundle under the other, a brass cage with two canaries dangling from a forefinger.

"I had to stop and catch one of the birds to put it in the cage with the other one," he explained the delay. "The darned thing broke away from me. That's why I was so long. Which'll you have? Take your pick."

For just an instant their eyes met and smiled together over the odd assortment. Then Jean plucked the cat from under his arm and set it before her in the saddle.

"Give me the birds while you mount," she said. "Hawk's been that wild to be going, you'll want your two hands, I'm thinking."

Without a word he surrendered the cage, and with a lightning wrap and two swift yanks of the saddle strings, tied on the bundle. Then Than was on and reaching for the birdcage, Jean gathered the cat under one arm and they galloped away down the creek to Dade's place.

The fire came snapping after them, but the mown meadow starved it to half the ferocity it had shown in Than's pasture. They left the horses in Dade's corral, set the birdcage in his cabin, gathered more grain sacks and more buckets of water, and stubbornly renewed the battle well above his buildings and the unguarded stacks. Working like mad, they started a backfire, whipped out the blaze on the lower side, coaxed it to eat its way up the valley. Rod by rod they lengthened their guard; from creek to the cabin and beyond. As far as they dared go with any hope of controlling it, they laid a charred barrier in the path of that devouring red wave rolling down across the fields.

Pitifully narrow, that barrier, for their time was short and the whooping wind fought back their creeping line of flame. They could not save both cabin and stacks, for

Dade had built them too far apart; and thinking of his mother and Susan, Than had made his choice. Hay would not be needed for a month or two yet, and it could be bought and hauled in. A cabin would take time to build and the nights were cold.

Even so, the odds were against saving the cabin and stable. Than brought more water, set the buckets at either end of their guard. Jean at the far end, Than at the closest and most critical point, they dipped their sacks in, carried them dripping to their stations behind the slowly widening black line, and waited, facing the smoke that half suffocated them, the heat that seemed to sear their very blood.

Jean swayed like a drunken man as she stood, the wet sack making a little puddle under the drip. Her arms were sticks, dead things attached to her body. But to Than, watching her anxiously through the smoke, she seemed tireless, invincible. The amused smile in her eyes when she reached down for the cat was the look he fancied was in them still. Jean, with her teasing Scotch accent, which he suspected was half put on for effect; Jean with her heather-blue eyes and the lilt in her voice; Jean with the ripe red lips—kissed by her sweetheart, Frank Hoskins.

A sick wave of hopelessness swept Than's nerves, set them jangling. His flesh crept with a chill of defeat. A burning twig, falling at his feet, pawed with spiteful yellow catclaws of flame at the grass. With a vicious blow the wet sack came down. Three tiny wisps of smoke rose, whipped away on the wind and were gone.

The fight was on.

CHAPTER ELEVEN

"WILL YOU LOOK AT THAT!" BESIDE DADE'S WELL, A half-emptied tin cup in her hand, Jean nodded toward the east. "There's another fire away down there!"

Than peered with smarting red-rimmed eyes. "Your eyesight's better than mine," he said. "The smoke's so thick you could cut it with a knife—"

"It's a different color next the ground. They're setting another backfire down there by Dade's cornfield."

Than gave a snort and swung a bucket under the pump spout. "That's swell. Now we'll get some more gentle exercise. The darned chumps, why didn't they hustle up here and get busy? We could have saved Dade's hay, if we'd had some help."

"They'd be coming too late, perhaps. What exercise do you mean?"

Than gave her a grim smile. "Just another little backfire on our hands. We've got this one headed on past, and now they're sending another one straight up the creek. We've got to set one to meet that." Suddenly his tone changed to a brusque tenderness. "You go in the shack with the birds and cat and lie down. You're about all in, right now. I can handle this alone. The wind's in our favor." He laid a hand on her shoulder. "Go on— please! You've done the work of two men already."

"And if another should be needed, I can do the work of three." She bent stiffly, picked up her draggled sack, and was ready to start.

"Go on— before I pack you in and lock the door on you."

"Ye wull not! Come away and stop your foolishness. We'll start our fire and then we both can rest."

"Say, did any one ever tell you you're stubborn as a team of mules?" Than watched her while he pumped the two buckets full.

"Mony's the time, an' I telt them it wasna stubbornness but a braw deetairmination tae see a thing through tae the end."

Than's arms tensed, aching to reach out, take her and hold her close. But he thought of Frank Hoskins and reached for the two buckets of water instead.

"All right, pick up my sack then and carry it out for me," he said, with a short laugh. "You and that braw deetairmination of yours sure will get your fill of fighting fire before you see this job ended."

Opposite the shack he set down the buckets, turned and went inside, came out with the brown cloth bundle. Awkwardly he thrust it at Jean.

"Better get into this riding skirt of Sue's. We're liable to have callers before long." Without looking at her, he picked up the buckets and went on.

A hot flush surged into Jean's face. All through that desperate battle to save his home and his mother's—all their most prized possessions—she had not once thought of her bloomered legs, unmaidenly as such exposure was considered in the Nineties. Not by the slyest sidelong look had Than betrayed any consciousness of her unprecedented appearance. But he had noticed it, nevertheless. Even in that wild rush to save the most vital things he had remembered to borrow a skirt from Susan.

Jean gulped down a sob or two while she stepped into the skirt, fumbled hooks and eyes, buckled her belt trimly into place, hiding the skirt band. Her tears were not tears of anger; Jean did not quite know why she cried.

She was not crying when she overtook Than, though the marks were on her face. She came up beside him, trying to seem unconcerned. "I never guessed I was such a bean pole, until I got into Susan's clothes."

"Sis always was runty," Than said, without looking at her. "What d' you think? This potato patch oughta save us some work. Here are some matches—you might start'er burning down along here. Good thing Dade started along this edge to dig his spuds. I'll start over there, in the grass. It won't take us long. We'll have a complete circle around Dade's buildings."

He went off, carrying one of the buckets and trailing his gunnysack over the rough ground. Unaccountably Jean wanted to cry again for no reason whatever, but she set to work starting little fires in the tangled dry grass at the edge of the fresh-ploughed ground. After the terrific ordeal of the past two hours, this was child's play. She felt very prim and ladylike in Susan's Sunday-best riding skirt, even if it was a good four inches too short. She had no idea that her face looked like a lady fireman just come out of a stokehole, nor that her forty-dollar Stetson was scorched in a dozen places where sparks had lived long enough to burn the fine gray felt.

Than dragged his burning grass tufts well out to where the great fire had swept past, then fought it from creeping back against the wind. Abruptly he threw down the tattered fragment of sack, poured out the little water left in the bucket and came over to meet Jean. He looked haggard, years older in the last two hours, and his mouth was hard.

"Let 'er flicker," he said apathetically. "I've shot my bolt—I pass 'er along to the Tepee with my regards."

Jean sent a troubled glance behind her where the world seemed all on fire. "Father has kept his guards clean of grass all summer. Our ranch is safe, I think." She looked at Than, hesitating to speak what was in her mind.

"Oh, I know!" he said bitterly, answering her thought. "If I'd burned my fireguards, we wouldn't have lost about everything we've got in the world. Well, I didn't. The wind's been blowing every day for a month and I've had the work on two ranches to do. There's only one of me—" He broke off, then added, "I seem to be about half a man, at that."

"If you're wanting me to contradict that, I can not do it. I'm that tired! And I've been wanting to ask you where are all the folks, Than?"

"Gone to Chinook. Mom had Dad's soldier right, so her time's served here. She proved up on her homestead yesterday. They took both teams, thank the Lord; saved wagons and two dandy sets of harness, anyway. Otherwise we'd be strapped for something to haul lumber—And I offered to stay and look after things! Fine job I made of it, I must say!"

"Noo, dinna reproach yersel', laddie. Barrin' the wee bit mistake ye made when ye rode inta thae gully and didna ride oot again with due expedeetion, ye made a braw ficht o't."

Than swung his slack shoulders toward her, looking half smiling, trying to meet her eyes.

"You're some braw yourself, if anybody should ask. If you could talk Scotch as well as you can fight fire, your dad would be setting up nights, practicing how to roll his r's so as to beat yours."

"Weel, if ye dinna like the way I speak tae ye—"

"I like the *way* all right. But I dinna know what

91

you're talking about."

"As for instance?"

"As for me riding into a gully and not riding out. Is that just Scotch talk, or what?"

"It is what I should like you to explain, if you please."

"Explain? Good glory! I don't even know what you're driving at, Jean. The only gully I rode into was that burned-over one I had to cross getting down out of the hills. I rode up there to take a look at our cattle we put in that first meadow up there last spring; and I wanted to get a line on some timber we could cut for posts next winter; and to see about a better trail to haul wood down. Lord, I had a lot of looking around to do up there! But when I saw the smoke boil up over the trees, I beat it down to see what was going on."

Jean found she was still carrying the soggy black rag that an hour ago had been a clean yellow gunny sack, smelling pleasantly of ripe grain. She dropped it with a little sound of chagrin and looked up into Than's eyes.

"A man rode into the gully that crosses the road near the corner of your fence. I was watching to see him ride out, but he didna come. It was soon after that I discovered the fire, back up in the wide—"

Than's nod interrupted her. "I saw where it started, all right. I rode down the other side." They had reached the shack. He threw open the door, stood aside to let her pass in. "I'll start a fire and heat some water so you can wash up. And I guess some good hot coffee wouldn't do any harm, either."

"I should ride away home and let them know I'm safe," Jean demurred. But she sat down on a chest with cushioned lid and pulled off her hat. "I must be a sight!" she sighed, drawing a handkerchief down her cheek and bringing it away black.

Knife out, Than was whittling shavings from Dade's kindling stick. He looked up, his eyes rather intent. With an unforeseen impulse, he dropped the stick and came over and sat down beside her. He did not offer to slide an arm around her, even to take her hand. He leaned, still with that intent look in his eyes, and looked into hers, and he was so close he saw himself reflected in her pupils.

"You're black as a coal beaver, and you've been crying, but I think you're just about the loveliest thing God ever made. What you've done today I can't thank you—I haven't tried. Some things are too big for words. But you—I don't want you to think I—"

"Man, ye've no call to stutter over thanking me. Susan's my dearest friend in the world, and your mother's like my own to me. And could I do less than try to save their home for them?" She blinked, turned her face aside, biting her lips to steady them. "I could just as well have sat by and folded my hands, for all the good I did. But if ye feel ye must thank me, let it be with a good cup of coffee. I'm near famished." She got up and walked to the doorway, stood there looking out at the black desolation before her.

"Why, sure." Than got up, feeling rather foolish and as if he had somehow been put in his place.

"But good glory, Jean! You can't expect a fellow to take what you did and never say a word to show."

"You'll show it far better with the hot water and the coffee," she said glumly. "We both did our damnedest," she added, turning with a sudden smile at him. "That, I'm thinking, is all a body is required to do." She took the tin dipper off its nail over the bucket, dipped water into the clean tin basin.

She laughed with the dry humor that was so much a

93

part of her. "That brother of yours would be sore vexed if he could see what this basin will look like when I'm through," she said. "I've never seen inside your shack, Than; but if you keep it as finicky as Dade keeps this one—"

"If I didn't, you'll never know it now," Than replied, bringing the teakettle over to be filled.

Something in his voice touched her. She laid a grimy hand on his arm. "You'll have a better house next time, Than," she said, and not many persons had ever heard her tone so gentle. "And maybe you'll build the new one back a little, so there'll be trees in the front of it. I know just the place, on that little knoll back in the edge of the grove. A beautiful cool place in summer and sheltered in winter from the north wind."

Than set the kettle on the stove and turned to Dade's cupboard, looking for food easily cooked. "I had to build down as close to my east line as I could, so as to be near Mom and Susan," he explained. But the site of his next house did not concern him much just then. He went silently about his work, frowning over some thought that held him from speech.

Jean had washed her face and was patting her hair into place with her fingers, pulling a pin out here and there, only to push it back in what seemed to be its original position. Her eyes were still red and her nose was frankly shiny—since nice girls did not use powder on their faces in those days. Than came and stood beside her, staring abstractedly out through the open doorway at the bleak bare field.

"You say you saw some one ride into that gully. Have you any idea who it was?"

"No. He was too far away, Than, and I only got a glimpse of him. He rode a dark horse brown or black, I couldn't tell which." She hesitated. "I thought at the time it might be you."

Than shook his head. "I was in the hills. I told you."

"Whoever it was, he set that fire. I'm sure of it." She gave Than an odd, searching look. "Have you been having trouble with some one?"

"Not a soul. Oh, Bearnson don't love us any too well, I guess. But he's never made a crooked move all the while we've been here. And you know how the boys have been. I'd hate to think one of them would pull a stunt like that." He looked at her inquiringly. "You suppose some darned chump dropped a match just by accident?"

"I do not. We'll have our coffee and a bite to eat and then we'll ride back up there and see what we can find out."

"Will you do that? Aren't you too tired?"

Jean turned to stove and cupboard, briskly finishing Than's hasty preparations for a meal. "I'm not too tired to find out who set that fire," she said grimly.

But after all, she did not go. They were no more than half through with their makeshift meal when some one came galloping into the yard, flung himself off his horse in a hurry and strode up to the door just as Than reached it, wiping his mouth with one of Dade's best napkins which he had found put away in a trunk.

Frank Hoskins, pale under his tan, opened his mouth to speak, then closed it to swallow dryly when he saw Jean MacHardie sitting inside, calmly drinking her second cup of coffee.

"Is it you, Frank!" Jean greeted him cheerfully in her most tantalizing Scottish voice.

"Jean! Thank the Lord I've found you—safe!" Frank brushed past Than and bent over her, looking as though

95

he meant to kiss her, regardless of Than's presence. "Dear, you gave me a scare! Your horse came home with empty saddle. What happened to you?"

Jean set down her cup and rose, looking around for her hat. "And what could happen, but a walk home? I came to see Susan, but she wasna home, so I rode a wee bit farther into the hills. And when I was off Robin, he chose that time to run away home. I was just about borrowing Susan's horse, but if you've brought Robin, there's no need. And what of the fire, Frank? Is it burning still?"

Altogether a different Jean, Than thought, as he watched the two. Engaged, from the look of things. She hadn't a glance or a word for him now that Frank was there. She seemed to forget all about going to see just how that fire had been started, or what had become of the man who had disappeared so mysteriously in the gully. While they ate, she had talked about it, had seemed terribly anxious to find out just where the fellow had gone. Terribly anxious—until Frank showed up.

Yet he had to admit that it was perfectly natural. If he were engaged to a girl, he certainly would expect her to show some interest when he was around. He wouldn't expect her to go riding off with another fellow, looking for tracks or anything else.

For all that, the sight of the two riding away together added considerably to the gloom that settled upon him when he rode back across the burned pasture, going alone to the place where the disaster planned for the Roberts family had been launched.

CHAPTER TWELVE

FAR OFF IN THE SMOKE-TAINTED DUSK SOUNDED THE cluck of loaded wagons pulling up the last long hill before the road they would take turned off the highway. Black Hawk threw up his head, listened intently with his ears tilted forward, sent an abrupt whinny toward the sound. A thrill of dread that was like physical nausea swept over Than, the dread of that dismal home-coming. But he set his teeth together and rode toward the sound.

Soon he could see the first wagon, a vague moving shape against the hillside. He heard voices, a man's laugh with a wooing note in it. His heart gave a throb of pleased surprise. He loped forward.

"That you, Blaney? Where'd you drop down from?"

"Oh, I ran across a bunch of strays over in the land office at Chinook. Thought I'd bring 'em in and maybe claim a reward."

Again that laugh with the indefinable wooing note of a man in love. Susan's shy giggle gave the answer to any question there might have been in Than's mind. But Than had no thoughts for Blaney's love-making just then, nor for Susan's apparent acquiescence. In one divining flash he had caught their mental picture of their homecoming; the glow of lamplight on the log walls hung with old-fashioned pictures in gilt frames; the table spread in the big kitchen with Mom's best tablecloth and china; appetizing odors; the crackle of paper as mysterious packages were being unwrapped; every one laughing, wanting to talk, trying to get a word in edgewise; Blaney across the table, his eyes swinging toward Sis every minute or so; food and warmth and

97

happy clamor, and Mom wanting to know how many eggs Than had gathered and had he saved a churning of cream.

"Had a fire down this way, didn't you, Than? We saw a big smoke, but it looked to be north of here. Do any damage?"

"Well, I guess it did about all there was to do. Sure didn't skip much." Than's voice coming through the dusk sounded harsh, almost repellent.

He saw Blaney lean toward him. "What's that? You don't mean—"

"I sure do. We're burnt out. Slick and clean! All but Dade's shack and stables. You'll have to drive on down there, Blaney. Mom and Sis can have Dade's bed. We'll sleep out, to-night."

"Oh! My piano—and *everything?*" wailed Susan.

"Well, I got your cat out all right, Sis. Both your canary birds too. Took 'em down to Dade's; I better go back and tell Mom."

He heard Susan crying as he reined Hawk away from the wagon; heard Blaney's voice, coaxing, comforting. Good thing Blaney happened to come along; must have spunked up courage to pop the question. Got the answer he wanted, by the look of things.

Funny. Mom seemed to know what it was he had to say. Like Blaney, she leaned out toward him and spoke into the dusk as he came up to the wagon.

"That you, Jonathan? You don't have to tell me—I know. Old Pete Bearnson's went to work and burnt us out."

"How'd you hear?"

"I didn't have to hear. Soon as we seen the smoke, as we was coming out of Camas, I said to David, 'Old Pete's gone on the warpath and started a prairie fire,' I says, 'meaning to burn us out. And with this wind blowing straight out of the west,' I says, 'he'll more'n likely accomplish his purpose.' Did you manage to save anything at all, Thannie?"

"Your deed box and the cat and the two canary birds is all from your place. I ducked in and got some papers I had—filing papers and some bills of sale. Jean MacHardie happened along and she helped me backfire. We saved Dade's buildings but the hay and everything else went up in smoke."

"Well, that's better'n I really expected," Mom declared, in a tone of relief. "What about the chickens an' pigs an' things? Any of them left?"

In the twilight she could see Than's head move sidewise. "I don't know about the chickens, Mom. That old black sow managed to root her way under the pen again and the whole shooting match got out this morning. Maybe they swam the creek; I didn't see any of them around. The fire didn't jump the creek—wind carried it straight down our side. The ducks and geese made it all right, I think. Lucky we had all the stock over in the north pasture—"

On the high spring seat Mom squared her shoulders. "That ain't luck, Jonathan, that's foresight. I've been suspicioning something was about due to happen. You recall the Tepee boys ain't been over lately—"

"They're all out on round-up, Mom. They wouldn't do a thing like this, anyway."

"Don't you be too sure about what they'd do!" cried Mom, ready for battle. "They're in the pay of old Pete, every last one of 'em. I mistrust that outfit and I always have . . ."

"Well, I'll go on ahead and get a fire started. I expect you're all about half-starved," Than told them, and sent

Hawk past the plodding team and into the trail ahead.

He took a short-cut down off the hill, avoiding the lead wagon with Blaney and Susan, who would only feel his presence an interruption. As he rode out upon the ink-black area where the fire had passed, the charred stubble crunching faintly under Hawk's feet seemed to him the most desolate sound he had ever heard in his life. Nearly two years of labor had gone up in smoke. Cattle, horses to feed through the winter, and no hay. Frosty nights already upon them and no roof to cover him. The prospect looked bleak enough that night.

Yet, because his imagination reached out to the others and the terrific shock this must be to them, Than presently shook himself out of his own bitter mood and galloped on ahead to Dade's cabin. He lighted Dade's largest lamp with its meticulously polished chimney and set it before the west window, where it would shine a welcome. He cleared Dade's reading table and put it in the middle of the room, brought out all the dishes Dade had and arranged them according to a man's idea of harmony. He made a big batch of biscuits, sliced as many onions and potatoes as the frying pan would hold, salted and peppered them lavishly and set them on the hottest part of the stove to fry. He opened cans with a reckless prodigality, for once thankful for Dade's finicky appetite and his proclivity for indulging his sweet tooth. He had a real range banquet in preparation when the two wagons stopped in front of the cabin. Than went out, lifted his mother down from the high seat.

"You and Sis can get the grub on to the table, Mom. I'll unhitch. And say! Keep an eye on the biscuits, will you?" He turned to Dade. "You go on in. I'll put up the team."

Habit was asserting itself: the habit of taking the brunt of things and saving Dade wherever he could. Blaney was unhitching the other team, his figure a dim shape in the murky starlight. Dade hesitated, said all right, and turned away. And that too was habit.

Mom appeared in the doorway, her black velvet bonnet with its three ostrich tips dangling by its watered-silk ribbon from her hands. "See if you can find that box I put that bag of apples in, David. And them cans of oysters too. Thannie's went to work and fixed us up a real company supper, and I guess we might as well have some oyster soup to go with it. It'll maybe help to kinda take the edge off our trouble. Oh, the crackers are right in that same box with the oysters an' apples."

"What're you going to make the soup of, Mom?" Than called out banteringly, as he unhooked the neck yoke and let down the wagon tongue. "There isn't any milk, remember."

"Why? D' you mean to tell me 't my milk house burned? I don't see how it could, dug in over the spring as it is, and a dirt roof—"

"Well, maybe not. Get me a lantern and bucket and I'll ride up and find out. There's no milk down here, though; that's a cinch."

Mom spoke over her shoulder. "Light the lantern, Baby, and bring Jonathan a clean lard bucket with a lid on. 'Twon't take but a minute or two for him to ride up there, and I've got my mind set on havin' them oysters. If we don't need 'em tonight, I don't know when we ever will."

"I'll ride up with you," Blaney offered, as Than turned the harnessed teams into the corral and led out Hawk. "I'll go get my horse."

With lantern and bucket, Than waited until Blaney

101

rode up beside him and reached out for the lantern, blowing it out with one breath as they swung into the ash-covered trail. They galloped off, neither speaking until they had dismounted beside the spring house. A few rods away, embers of logs winked like red eyes in the darkness; thin streamers of smoke curled away before the failing breeze. Blaney struck a match and lighted the lantern again. Than took it, pulled open the scorched door of stout planking that closed the dugout.

Brown stone crocks of milk stood half-submerged in the shallow pool hollowed out from the spring. On some the cream was wrinkled, the surface glazed. Than held the lantern tilted so that the light shone upon the pool, made his choice and gave the lantern to Blaney.

"They overlooked a bet here," he said somberly, as he stooped and lifted a crock. "If they knew, I expect they'd sneak over and wreck this place too." He set the bucket down and tilted the crock over it, pouring slowly so that the rich yellow cream slid over the edge. When the surface showed milky, he set down that crock and took up another. "Might as well stake ourselves to the best there is," he remarked, glancing up under his hatbrim at Blaney. "Anyway, the churn went up in smoke. Mom always kept it on the back porch in the sun."

"It's hell," said Blaney. "Coming so late, we'll have our hands full getting ready for winter."

"We?" Than pressed down the lid over the bucket and stood up, looking curiously at the other.

"You're darn right. Unless you tell me to get out." Blaney laughed a little as he turned to lead the way out with the lantern. "I've quit the land business. Or I'm going to. Thought maybe you'd let me in with you, Than. I've got a little money I could put into cattle, on any basis you want."

Than walked to his horse before he spoke. When he did, his voice was grave. "Yesterday I'd have been tickled to death, Blaney. Tonight's a horse of another color." He mounted carefully, reined Hawk back into the trail. "They waited a long time to start in on us, but they sure landed with all four feet when they did start. You see what happened."

"Couldn't it have been an accident?" Blaney sent his horse up alongside Than.

"Yeah," Than answered dryly. "It could—but it wasn't. Not by a damn sight."

"You don't think it was the Tepee, do you?"

"That's something to figure out later."

Because of the milk, they were riding back more slowly than they had come. Blaney said nothing for a minute. "Any one else liable to do it?" he asked presently.

"Well, those homesteaders back here on Dry Creek don't like us any too well but I don't know as they'd carry a grudge far enough to burn us out. Dade had a run-in with Dahlburg over some stock that got through our fence and wound up down at Dade's place. Didn't amount to much, only it happened to be one of Dade's ornery days and he raised Cain. Went over there and picked a fight, judging by the shiners he brought home with him." Than gave a half-amused snort. "I didn't ask who did it, but I expect it was Dahlburg. He's big enough to whale the tar out of Dade. Those black eyes were lulus, all right."

"That doesn't sound as if he'd be out after more revenge," Blaney mused. "How long ago was that?"

"Oh, last spring sometime, when Dade was all enthused over raising corn. He had a patch over across

103

the creek and I guess Dahlburg's cattle sampled some of it; or he was afraid they were going to. I was over at the Tepee picking up a few head of our cattle they'd cut out of their bunch." His voice took a different note. "We branded forty-two calves last spring, Blaney. That isn't such a lot, but it's a start, anyway. I was going to throw them in the pasture here and start feeding hay the minute this warm spell was over. Now—"

"It sure is hell," Blaney repeated, because after all, those words seemed to express his feelings as well as any.

They were nearing Dade's cabin. They saw the door open, light stream out into the yard. Two men went in, the door closing behind them. With a common impulse, Than and Blaney sent their horses forward at a faster trot.

They were no more than two or three minutes behind the callers but already the atmosphere within the cabin had grown tense. Dade's cold incisive tones reached them as they approached the door . . . "—and we'll certainly even the score!"

Mom's voice rose with the heat of battle. "If you didn't do it yourselves, you're in the pay of the low-lived cur that did. And there's an old saying, 'You may as well eat the devil as drink his broth.' You're drinkin' devil's broth just as long as you hang around old Pete Bearnson."

"Well," Dilly retorted, "what do you want us to do? Quit our jobs just because you folks got burnt out?"

"Yeah, that'd be swell!" Rosy chimed in sarcastically.

Than pushed into the room and held out the bucket mechanically. "Here's your milk, Mom. Hello, boys. What's the argument?"

Dilly wheeled, his face red with anger. "I s'pose

you're another one that thinks we're the cause of all this." His head jerked toward the blackness outside. "Are you?"

"I haven't accused you yet, have I?"

"Not yet. And I don't see where any one's got the license to. We're working for Bearnson. That don't mean we're doing his dirty work."

"Oh!" Dade's tone was intolerably sneering. "Then you admit he is doing dirty work—such as setting prairie fires!"

"I don't admit anything of the kind." Dilly made angry denial.

"We're working for Bearnson and we ain't goin' to stand for any such talk, from you or nobody else!" Rosy broke in truculently. "We rode over here to see what damage was done and see if maybe we could do anything. We—"

"No, there's nothing more you can do!" Mom told him bluntly. "If it wasn't you personally, it was some of your outfit, and we're goin' to draw the line pritty sharp from now on."

"I s'pose that means git out," Rosy interpreted indignantly.

"You can take it any way you're a mind to."

Dilly brushed past Than and laid his hand on the door knob. "Come on, Rosy. Our room's better than our company here, I guess." He turned and sent a queer, hurt look around the group. "I'm sure glad to find out just what you folks think we're capable of," he said. "I s'posed all this time we was pretty good friends but I see I've got another think comin'." He went out into the night.

"Folks that's as suspicious as what you folks are, had *oughta* be burnt out!" Rosy flung a last bitter reproach

105

at them and waddled out after Dilly.

Than and Blaney looked at each other helplessly as the muffled cluppety-clup of swift hoofbeats vanished in the distance.

"Well, I don't care!" Mom defended her harshness. "I didn't say a thing to them I wouldn't say to old Pete himself; and I'm a-going to make it my business to tell him right to his face what I think of him." Her tone changed abruptly. "Baby, see if you can scare up bowls enough to dish up this soup. You boys set right down and start in and I don't want to hear a word more tonight about what's happened. Tomorrow's time enough to face it. I want you should enjoy these oysters now and the fine meal Thannie fixed up for us. Baby, you pour the coffee."

Which was all very well. But they couldn't forget the charred acres that had been three full harvested ranches that morning. And Than, at least, could not forget the friendships laid waste within that room.

CHAPTER THIRTEEN

WITH HIS BACK AGAINST THE PINE TREE JEAN HAD mentioned as a fine shade for the new cabin he must build, and with a camp fire burning just far enough away to avoid searing the lower branches of his tree, Than smoked and talked in low tones to Blaney rolled in a blanket beside him.

"I'd a heap rather sleep out under this tree than in Dade's stable with the horses," he explained speciously. "I think I'll put my cabin here. It's more sheltered. Had to get down close to my east line, before, on account of Mom and Susan, but they won't need me close, any more."

"Well, why not put up a good log house here, big enough for all of us? Unless," Blaney added quickly, "you'd rather have one just big enough for two."

Than missed his meaning. He frowned at the fire. "Of course, I'm tickled to death to have you in the family; you know that, Blaney. But I hate to have you buy into the game right now. Things are going to tighten around here, unless I'm badly mistaken."

"All the more reason why I want to be in on it."

"Yeah, I sabe that, all right. But there's the women to think of. Why don't you and Sis go ahead and get married and take Mom back to the Falls for the winter? There's nothing to keep them here, now Mom's proved up on her claim. They'd be a lot more comfortable and so would I. In my mind, anyway."

"Well, for one thing, Sue wouldn't want to do that. What she wants is to wait till spring and then maybe we could have a double wedding."

"Hunh?" Than pulled himself straighter against the tree. "She's crazy with the heat. Dade's girl is up in the Falls, and anyway, they've had a scrap and the engagement is called off, from what Dade let out. There's nobody to double up with."

Blaney lifted his head off his arm and looked at Than. "Well, how about you and that Scotch lassie down the creek?"

"Say! Who's been stringin' you?"

"I didn't think anybody was. Last spring when I was down here you sure had all the earmarks, boy. I'd have bet money you were spreading your loop for the Scotch girl. And Sue says—"

"Sue talks a lot just to hear herself," Than declared with true brotherly frankness. "Jean MacHardie's a fine girl, but I haven't—my rope's coiled and tied to the saddle, far as she or any other girl's concerned. I've got no time for a wife," he stated with careful emphasis. "And furthermore, Frank Hoskins happens to have his loop on her. They're engaged."

"The devil they are! Frank, hunh? I knew they used to go together a little, back a couple of years ago. But Sue —"

"About half the time," Than said gruffly, "Sue talks through her hat. You take my advice, Blaney, and let most of what Sis tells you go in one ear and out the other. What she don't know about Jean MacHardie would make a book, and I don't give a darn if they are always chumming together."

"Well, of course," Blaney admitted with caution, "you ought to know your own mind if anybody does."

"And what's more, I know hers. Jean and Frank were up here today—helped with the fire. Any fool could see they're crazy about each other. You might," Than added, with a hard little laugh, "frame up a double wedding with them. But from the looks of things, you'd have to get a move on or they'll beat you to it."

"Well, I don't know about that. I thought it'd be in the family—"

"Then you talk to Dade about it. But he's quit writing to his girl, so it looks to me like your chances are pretty darn slim." Than tossed his cigarette stub into the flames. "It would simplify matters a lot, Blaney, if you and Sis got married right away and took Mom back to town with you. They won't want to crowd in on Dade for any length of time, and to build a house for them that they could winter in comfortably—and haul out furniture —"

"I could do all that."

"Well, but I'm liable to have a fight on my hands before this thing's settled. I hope you don't think I'm going to take this lying down. Do you?"

"Well, I never knew you to lie down on a job yet—or a fight, either. That's why you need somebody with you. You don't seem to count much on Dade, I notice."

"No, I don't. I can't, Blaney. I've got a temper myself, but I do try to keep the upper hand on it. Dade spits out just whatever comes into his head when he's mad and you never know what minute he'll blow up. You know. You got a sample."

"You mean away back when we located here?"

"Well, that's one time. He's been on the outs with the Tepee boys ever since. Just barely civil when he's in a good humor. And you heard him tonight. Mom too. She's always liked Dilly and Rose and the rest, but you heard how she turned on 'em tonight. With Mom to egg Dade on, there's no telling what he might do. Go over and burn out the Tepee, maybe. It would be about his idea of playing even. If I could get Mom away from here before things come to a showdown, I can maybe handle Dade."

Blaney rolled over on his side, and with his head supported on his hand, he stared at the moon just rising over the low ridge beyond the MacHardie ranch. At another time his thoughts would have clung to love and Susan. Even now he wondered if she saw the moon, magnified as it was by smoke so that it looked like a huge round shield beaten out of copper.

But even love must wait upon warfare and presently his glance swung to Than's moody profile. "What makes you think it was the Tepee outfit that burned you out, Than?"

Than drew in his breath, seemed to be choosing

109

words. But he did not speak, after all, and Blaney added what was in his mind.

"Of course, I may be wrong. I haven't been here all the while and I don't know all that's happened. But tonight my sympathy was with Dilly and Rose. It didn't seem to me necessary to jump on them the way Dade and Mom did."

"It wasn't. That's what I mean when I wish Mom would go back to town. She and Dade are an awful lot alike in some ways. When they've got anything on their chest, all hell can't keep 'em from telling the world, if the notion strikes them that way. And of course, then I have to back them up more or less. I hated like the very devil to hear them light into Dilly that way, but—well, the Robertses have got to hang together."

"You don't think Dilly or Rosy knew anything about it, do you?"

"The fire? No-o, that's hard to say. I don't think *they* set it. They may not know just who did. Some one in the outfit, though. I'd bank on that, almost. Unless," he added, as an afterthought, "it might have been Dahlburg; and the evidence—what little I've got— points more to the Tepee."

"Yeah?"

"I don't want the folks to know it, Blaney. What I want to do is lie low till I find out for sure and then go after 'em with the sheriff to back me up. I want the pay for our buildings and for over two hundred tons of hay. You hit a man's pocket and he's *hurt,* what I mean. That's how I'm hurt and that's the way I'll hit back. Then," he added, with an acrid humor, "I may take the interest out of his hide."

"You've got some evidence, you say?"

A leaping flame sent its reflection to dance on Than's

face. The fitful play of light and shadow gave him a look of tortured mirth, Blaney thought; as if he were suffering and laughing at his own pain.

But his voice was steady, even to the point of being colorless. "You know that deep draw—call it a gully—that runs across up here, about halfway between the gate and the corner of the Tepee fence? The road crosses it. Well. It just happened that Jean MacHardie was riding up into the hills—or on the first ridge—just before the fire broke out in a little coulee over there."

"I know the place. I jumped a flock of sage chickens in there last fall. Remember?"

"Uh-hunh. That's the one. Well, see what you make of this. She saw a man ride into the end of that gully, where it peters out near the mouth of that hollow. She said she wondered who it was and she watched for him to come out, but he didn't. It was right after that the fire broke out."

"She couldn't tell who it was, though, you say."

"No. But listen here, Blaney. Before dark, I made it my business to take a look in that gully. Except where our road crosses it, a man can ride out of sight for over four miles, did you know that? He can ride," Than detailed, "from within a quarter of a mile of that little coulee to Running Man, where it makes that big bend south to the Tepee headquarters; within a few miles of their corrals."

"Is that right!"

"You're darned tooting it's right. And some bashful individual did ride that way. Round trip, up to the hills and back down again. I trailed him to the creek and lost his tracks there where stock has been watering all fall. But if I could have followed them, I'll bet they'd have led me straight to the Tepee corral."

111

"Hell!" said Blaney, in a shocked tone.

"Of course, I haven't any way right now of proving that man set the fire. But when you consider the fact that he let down a panel of Tepee fence where it crosses the gully and mended it after himself with a hammer and fresh staples, I'd say that gully riding was pretty damned premeditated."

"Sure looks that way," Blaney admitted.

"He rode a dark horse, Jean said. But that don't mean a thing. Every fellow in the outfit has got dark horses in his string and he'd sure pick one for a job like that. I thought they were all off on round-up, which would kinda let them out. But when I saw the boys, I knew the round-up had got in—so there's no telling who did it."

"The Tepee shipped out from Camas this morning," Blaney observed, yawning in spite of his intense interest in the subject. "I didn't see the boys to talk to them; couldn't say whether they were all there or not. Just saw a bunch of beef being loaded out and asked whose it was. They said the Tepee. That's all I know. That," he added, "was about ten o'clock."

"A man on horseback could make it across country in three hours, easy. I rode it in less time than that, last winter, when Dade came down with grippe. We thought it was pneumonia for a while." Than sighed. "I sure rode!"

"Dade don't look so good," Blaney commented.

"Better not tell him that. Better not say anything about that man riding the gully, either. Don't tell Sis, will you, Blaney? She'd spill it to Mom and she'd tell Dade—" He threw out a hand expressively.

"Sweet little old lady with feathers on her bonnet," Blaney mused. "To hear you talk, she's a holy terror."

Than grinned reluctantly. "Mom still thinks this is

Injun country and she'll have to shoot her way out before she's through with it. Fact. You may not believe it, but Mom sleeps every night of her life with a loaded shotgun standing at the head of her bed. Loaded with buckshot. And don't ever think she wouldn't blaze away with it, if she thought there was any good reason." He swallowed. "I mean she did have one. I bet she'll send for another right off to take its place."

Blaney yawned again. "Battle won't take place to-night, anyway. Better get yourself some sleep. As Mom said, tomorrow's time enough to face things. Lord, it's been a long time since I slept out like this." He wriggled hips and shoulders into an easier position in the thick carpet of pine needles. "Y'oughta be thankful, boy, that fire didn't get into this grove!"

"I am." Than added mentally, "*She* likes this spot."

He got up, dragged a broken branch to the fire, heaved one end full across the coals and went back to the place he had chosen close to the tree. In a cradled nook between two uncovered roots he spread the heavy Canadian wool blanket borrowed from Dade and lay down, wrapping the soft gray folds snugly around him.

But for a long, long while he did not close his eyes. The copper-brown moon, wading higher through the hazy night, wove a lacy pattern of drooping branch tips across her face. The fitful breeze played with it, changing the design with vagrant artistry as the moon drew upward behind thicker branches.

Than's shuttling thoughts wove their own invisible pattern as he gazed. Jean, all unconscious of his nearness, standing silhouetted against smoke and flame, beating, bending, moving a step and whipping the flames down with her skirt. Jean at the gate, waiting for him; the feel of her strong soft arms around him as they

113

galloped together down the pasture, racing the flames. Jean staggering toward him, carrying two slopping buckets of water, her smudged face drawn with worry and exhaustion . . . Jean freshened and smiling, looking up into Frank Hoskins' eyes while she burred her r's in the impishly fascinating way she had . . . The black wasteland stretching out from the knoll where he lay, and the winking glow of embers that were all that remained of his toilsome building of stables, cabins, corrals. Even the chicken house . . .

Oddly there flashed before him the picture of Mom's hens, running with spread wings and yellow legs twinkling, making for the brush which would presently be a roaring furnace about them. He groaned and shut his eyes, trying to dispel that poignant memory, but others came to take its place. The calf Jean had pushed from the stable; the last Than remembered, it was galloping awkwardly down toward Dade's place. Dead now, of course.

With the dawn would come plans, courage to build anew; but that night Than was far from feeling himself a phoenix; his thoughts could not rise above the ashes.

CHAPTER FOURTEEN

DADE SMILED DISAGREEABLY. "YOU CERTAINLY HAVE got old Job backed off the map. All you need now is a few boils on your neck and you'd be the original—"

"David, you can't make light of the Scriptures in that manner," his mother sharply reproved him. "I won't have it."

Dade slanted his smile toward her. "There's nothing Scriptural about Than. He's just plain foolish. Wants us to pass up this outrage; let them get away with it." He turned on Than. "Any darned one of those Tepee boys could walk up to you and plant a bullet in your liver and you'd refuse to believe he meant any harm by it," he said. "You can pass this up, if you like. I intend to take whatever action I see fit."

"You had no call to insult Dilly the way you did last night," Than insisted. "Nor Rosy either, for that matter. They—"

"That little sawed-off four-flusher? You couldn't insult him. Impossible."

"You haven't been around with those boys as much as I have," Than persisted, talking for Mom's benefit as much as Dade's. "If you want a line on a man's character, just ride on round-up with him and you'll get it. The Tepee boys have been riding over here off and on ever since we came and you don't know them a darned bit better than that first day when you made a fool of yourself and wanted to kill them, just for a grandstand show."

"If I had, we'd have our hay now," Dade sneered.

"If you had, you wouldn't be here now, you mean. But that's been your attitude from the start. You don't really know a single man or woman in this country. You've turned up your nose at the whole bunch and flocked off by yourself, too good to be civil. There ain't a man in the country you've taken the trouble to make friends with, unless it's Frank Hoskins, and you wouldn't have taken up with him if he didn't know about music and hadn't read enough Shakespeare to murder a few quotations. Maybe Dilly and little Rosy don't read anything much besides the papers, and they couldn't keep a set of books to save their lives, but they're *men.* They suit *me,* do you hear? I want you to

115

leave 'em alone."

Dade turned and looked out of the window at the bleak prospect up toward his mother's claim and Than's. He waved a hand ironically. "I suppose *that* suits you too!" he observed sarcastically.

"Boys, boys, I won't have you quarreling at the table! My good land, haven't we got trouble enough without you two getting at loggerheads over it?"

Than pushed back his chair. "All right, Mom. If you'll excuse us, Blaney and I have a little riding to do this morning."

"You're excused, Jonathan. You go on and turn your other cheek, if that's the way you feel about it, but I must say I agree with David. Old Pete Bearnson has got to meet his come-uppance. There's a law in this country and he's goin' to find it out."

"Good glory, Mom! You've never had any proof yet that this Bearnson is the old Pete you're always talking about. This Bearnson never has made a move against us, all the time we've been here. Give the devil his due, anyway."

"I'll give him his due, don't you worry a mite about that," Mom retorted and clicked her teeth, as she always did when her mouth closed quickly. "I've got the proof of my own eyes and that's plenty good enough for me, Jonathan. I met 'im face to face in Camas, yestiddy morning, and if he ain't the same old Pete Bearnson that used to skin people with that store of his in Helena twenty year ago, he's Pete's twin brother—and the good Lord never made two of *him*."

"All right, I'll take your word for it, Mom. Come on, Blaney, let's go."

"Right on the warpath, all right," Blaney grinned, when they were riding back up the trail.

116

"I'll say she is! You see now why I didn't want either of them to know about that gully rider. If Mom heard about that, she'd be rustling another shotgun somewhere so she could go over and fill Bearnson's hide with buckshot."

But he did not know his mother as well as he imagined. She did not need to hear about the man who rode along the gully and she did not need a shotgun (though she did wish that she had it). She waited only long enough to mix her bread and change into her best dress, and then she drove away with Dade to the Tepee ranch for the sole purpose of giving old Pete Bearnson a piece of her mind.

Back in the edge of the hills, Blaney and Than rode higher up the ridge where Jean had been when the fire started. Their immediate object was to see for themselves just how the land lay, looking down from that vantage point. With scarcely a deviation, Than had instinctively followed Jean's trail to the ledge and stopped.

"Here's about where she saw him," he said, dismounting at the spot. "You can see where her horse stood and here are her tracks in the dirt." They had not been talking of Jean; a small detail which Than overlooked, his thoughts were so full of her.

Blaney held back a smile. "All right, we'll sit down here a minute and size up the situation. You say the fire started over there."

"That little hump right over there is where this ridge drops down into the coulee." He pointed down to the right of them. "Right down there in the head of that gully; just the other side of the burned strip."

"That's where she saw him ride in, I take it."

"Yeah. It must be. You can see where it runs straight

to the road and the Tepee fence; and see how it goes on through to that bend in the creek? And every foot of it ridable in dry weather—" He broke off, squinting his eyes to stare fixedly at a moving dot a mile or more away.

"Looks like a team and wagon out there in the Tepee field. Good glory! Do you s'pose—? If it was Dade, he'd ride his sorrel. Do you s'pose Mom would take it into her head to drive over to the Tepee?"

Blaney gave a dry chuckle. "You heard her at breakfast. What do you think?"

Than scowled, watching the moving dot. "Well, I wouldn't put it past her." He turned and picked up Hawk's reins. "I better ride back down and see if she's home, Blaney. If she's gone over there and tangled with the Tepee, I'm going to take in after her."

They found Susan at Dade's cabin. With her sleeves rolled above her elbows and a smudge of flour on her nose, she was kneading down a puffy batch of bread dough. With one arm she brushed a strand of curly hair off her forehead and wrinkled her nose at Blaney, who walked up and kissed her shamelessly on her mouth.

Than mentally dismissed the two from his mind. Mom was not there; that was what counted. He turned and went out, leaving the two blissfully engaged in a make-believe argument at the table. Blaney in a lovesick guise chilled him somehow. He would not own to it, yet he must have known that it was because he hated to be reminded of Frank Hoskins and Jean, laughing together over trivial things in that room while tragedy held the place in its grip. He surely was glad he was not in love, he told himself viciously. If he ever was, and acted that silly, he hoped to the Lord some one would brain him with an ax and put him out of his misery.

He had reached the gully over in the Tepee field when Blaney came galloping furiously to overtake him.

"You going to follow these tracks around?" Blaney asked unnecessarily, since Than was already turning into that secret way.

"Why not? I don't want to advertise to Mom that I'm on her heels," Than countered shortly. Then he added in a more amiable tone, "It's about as short as to follow the trail."

In that he was mistaken. Mom had arrived and had said her say, or most of it. In her best dress and her black velvet bonnet with its ostrich tips and the watered-silk ribbon tied in a prim bow under her chin, she stood holding her ruffled skirt pinched up at the side, out of the corral dust. Her other hand was raised, shaking a forefinger under Bearnson's nose.

"You can deny it till you're black in the face but you can't change my opinion one inch. I know you've been peaceable. I know you've never lifted a finger against us. I know you've let Jonathan ride on round-up with you and gether what few cattle we've got. I know all that, Pete Bearnson, and I know it's all been for a purpose." The click of her teeth emphasized the sentence as she turned her head impatiently to see who was distracting Bearnson's attention.

Bearnson nodded to Than, stepped forward and shook hands with Blaney. "Heard you were down here," he said, with a perfunctory cordiality. "Expect to stay long? Glad to have you put up here, any time. It must be rather crowded over at the Robertses just now. Anything we can do—" His light gray eyes turned upon Than. "If you need any hay, I can let you have a ton or two till you can haul in some. You can pay it back when you get a

119

new crop next summer."

While Than was choosing words for a civil reply, Mom moved decisively into the center of the group. "No, thank you, Mr. Pete Bearnson, we don't need hay that bad," she told him, with biting sarcasm. "We might find ourselves in the same boat with the Wilkersons, over in Helena. You offered them goods, you remember; you urged them to buy and keep on buyin', and take their own time to pay the bill—and you wound up by pickin' them to the bone. I was standing right by the courthouse steps when the sheriff sold the furniture you'd attached, after you foreclosed."

Bearnson turned his round head with its close-clipped, graying hair and hard red face. He looked at Mom through half-closed, fleshy lids. "I can't call a lady a liar," he said, "but I will say you're taking great liberties with the truth."

"What's that?" Than leaned to inquire, his attention having been diverted to Hawk's curious sniffings at the feathers on Mom's bonnet. "Will you kindly repeat what you just said to my mother?"

"He don't have to repeat it," said Mom crisply. "*I* heard it plain enough." And she drew back her hand and slapped Bearnson so smartly that her black kid glove split the full length of her palm. "I knew I'd bring you out into the open where I could get at you," she cried, with a click of her teeth, and before even Bearnson, who was closest, could move, she pulled out a quirt from some mysterious fold in her black silk skirt and proceeded to use it with vigor and a surprising degree of skill.

"Mom! Good glory!" Than threw himself from his horse and rushed up to her, reaching for the quirt.

She whirled and slashed him across the cheek.

120

"Jonathan, you mind your business!" Like an angry schoolmistress she followed Bearnson, darted out a hand and caught him by the collar and whipped him without mercy. "You waited till winter was comin' on––and then you took good care we was away from home before you had the nerve to burn us out!" she berated him between blows. "You always was a patient waiter. And you'll offer us *hay*, will you?"

"I didn't burn you out!" yelled Bearnson, trying to break loose. One arm was up, shielding his face. "Quit it, you hell-cat! pull her off, before I—"

"Mom!" With a livid welt showing, Than's face was white as he caught her by the shoulders. Blaney was rushing in, a glint of amusement in his eyes.

Than staggered from an unexpected blow behind the ear. Dade was clawing at him, pulling him back. "Let her alone, you damn fool! He's got it coming!"

Tepee cowboys came running from blacksmith shop, corral—even the cook rushed up to see the scrap. Mom gave one final, vicious blow that somehow caught Bearnson on the chin and drew blood.

Bearnson struck out, then, not caring who got in the way of his fist. It happened to land on Than, who was busy trying to wrest the quirt from Mom's hand without hurting her. She fought him like the old warrior she was. Not until Blaney took a hand was she subdued; and then it was a mere physical subjection. Her tongue no man could tame.

Afterward Than knew it had all happened very quickly. The audience had no more than arrived when it was all over and Mom was straightening her bonnet and surveying her work with a grim satisfaction that made even Than's lips twitch, angry though he was.

"It ain't half what you deserve, but maybe it'll cause

121

you to think twice before starting anything with the Robertses again," she said. "Come, David, I've got to get back and put my bread in the pans."

Bearnson gave her one baleful look and walked off to the house, presumably for court plaster to put on his chin. The cowboys hesitated, grinned furtively and went back to their work. Than and Blaney mounted without a word and rode off home, leaving Mom and Dade to follow.

"And now," Than said grimly, as he and Blaney rode off in the dust of the wagon, "there'll be hell to pay—and no pitch hot! If Bearnson ain't the one that burnt us out, Mom's put us all to the bad. He'll be down on us like a wolf."

CHAPTER FIFTEEN

A NOTICEABLE COOLNESS IN HER LOOK AND HER manner served notice to Than that his mother resented his attitude toward Bearnson and the Tepee boys. Just what he should have done that day she did not tell him in words, and probably it was largely what he failed to do that annoyed her most. He should have fought Bearnson or at least one or two of his men. That Dade had not done so she seemed to overlook. Dade was not strong and his cough had returned to harass him intermittently. She did not expect David to fight; but a tall, powerful fellow like Jonathan ought to have gumption enough to stand up to old Pete

This to Susan and Jean, that afternoon when Jean rode up to return Susan's riding skirt. To the girls Mom spoke her mind without stint. But to Than she said nothing at all, until one evening when the housing problem came up for discussion. There she took her stand at once and in a tone that admitted no argument.

"You needn't figure on putting up another house for me, Jonathan," she said bluntly. "My land's my own now and I can live on it or not, jes's I please. David'll build me on a room here, and Babe an' I'll stay right here and keep house for him till her and Blaney gets married, and then they can do as they're a mind to."

"I thought I could put up a log house on my place—"

"You can put up a brick-an'-stone mansion on your place for all I care," his mother retorted. "I won't live in it. I'm a-goin' to stay right here with David."

"I thought maybe you'd like to spend the winter in the Falls—"

Mom gave a contemptuous sniff. "You thought I'd run away from old Pete, mebby. Well, I ain't a-goin' to stir a step outa this valley till he's whipped an' begs fer mercy. I never run away from trouble yet an' I'm gettin' too old to start in now. You go right along and mind your own business an' plan for yourself. David and I'll get along." She sent a quick glance around the table, scanning faces shrewdly, looking for approval, perhaps.

Than's face reddened. "Suit yourself, Mom. If here's where you elect to stay, I'd better haul out a load of lumber for that addition, first thing. The hay can wait awhile."

"You'll do nothing of the kind. You get your winter's hay hauled and you'll have your hands full enough. David and I're going to town tomorrow for a load of stuff and I'll take care of the lumber. Mercy sakes! A body'd think, Jonathan, that I was on the shelf, the way you talk. You don't seem to reelize that I took right hold and did a man's work, buildin' a home in the wilderness—before I was as old as Babe, here. I was

123

perfectly capable of handling things on a ranch before you was born. And I don't think," she summed up, with a click of her teeth, "I don't *think* my mind is failin' any—or my strength, either. I can still turn off a good day's work, I notice. You mind your own affairs, Jonathan, and I'll mind mine."

"That suits me fine," Than lied, a fine white line around his tense mouth. "Just so I know where we stand."

Mom gave him a toss of her head. "I sh'd think you made that pretty plain, Jonathan, the other day," she flung at him. "I had it brought home to me before strangers that my own son ain't willin' to stand by me in a pinch. So f'm now on, I'll fight my own battles in my own way. And you," she added grimly, "can lay down an' let folks walk all over you if you're a mind to."

With a muttered "Excuse me," Than pushed back his chair. He lifted his hat down off a nail, flung his coat over his arm and turned to the door.

"Jonathan, where're you going? There's apple pie—"

"I'm going to mind my own affairs," Than said evenly. "And I'm a pretty good cook myself. I can make my own apple pie."

"Jonathan, you set right down an' behave yourself!"

But Jonathan heard only the beginning of that command. The rest was spoken to the closed door while he walked angrily down the path to the corral.

In a white heat of anger he harnessed his own big team of gentle brown mares, hitched them to the wagon he considered his own, saddled Hawk and tied up the reins to the saddle horn and drove away. As the wagon rolled away from the corral, he looked back. The door had opened, letting out a gush of yellow lamplight into the twilight. He saw Mom's wiry form outlined against the light within the doorway and he thought he heard her call to him. He faced front quickly, chirping to the team. They broke into a trot, drawing the empty wagon rapidly away over the hard-beaten trail up the creek.

Blaney would probably come after him, thinking he had gone up to his makeshift camp on the knoll under the pine tree. He did not want Blaney involved in this; Blaney, marrying Susan, would find life a lot easier if Mom were not prejudiced against him. Furthermore, Than wanted to settle this matter alone, without any advice or interference. Mom'd have to come around to the right attitude toward her neighbors and do it of her own accord. And Than, from now on, meant to be merely a neighbor and no more.

He kept straight on, through the outside gate and into the trail to town. He did not hurry the horses, but neither did he loaf along. He was only doing now what he had meant to do a little later on, he told himself. And if they wondered where he had gone, that was none of their business. Mom had served notice for the family. It did not lessen Than's bitterness that Dade had sat there passively acquiescent, with that twisted little smile that always made him look so superior and so sneering. No, he'd just go on about his own affairs, as Mom told him to do. She had Dade and Blaney. She sure didn't seem to need him any longer.

That night he drove to Camas, arriving long after every one was in bed. But the livery stable had a night bell and a yawning hostler came and took the sweaty brown mares in charge. In the nippy cold of the frosty starlight, Than walked back to the silent hotel, where a dim light burned over the desk and the night clerk dozed with his armchair tilted back against the wall between the safe and the bar.

125

He was an efficient old fellow who owned a third interest in the place and for that slept lightly as a wildcat. Than's step outside the door woke him. He offered Than a drink on the house, and when that was refused, he lifted a key off a hook and handed it over, together with a lamp which he obligingly lighted.

"Right on down the hall, last on your right," he gave perfunctory directions. "Want to leave a call for breakfast?"

"No," said Than, glancing at the clock. "I'll lay over tomorrow—or today, rather—and get an early start tomorrow. I'd like a bowl of bread and milk, if you've got the makin's handy, and then I'm liable to sleep till noon."

"How about cold corn bread? I always 'd ruther have cold corn bread an' milk than fried chicken, any day."

"You bet. And say, you needn't bother about skimming that milk. I can eat the skimmin's."

With a cackle of appreciation, the night clerk pushed through the yellow swinging doors into the dining room. His steps receded, another door swung on squeaky hinges. Presently he appeared, carrying a battered black serving tray on which were grouped two dingy tablespoons, two thick white bowls, a large glass pitcher of milk and a meat platter heaped with crumbly yellow squares of corn bread.

"Made me so dang hungry, cuttin' that johnnycake, I jest took a notion I'd have me a snack too," he chuckled apologetically. "Had m' cawfee an' san'wiches at midnight, but shucks! That was over two hour ago. I ain't goin' to set back droolin' at the mouth an' watch you eatin' johnnycake an' milk. I ain't never too full for a bowl of this stuff."

"Same here," grinned Than, and held a bowl while

126

the night clerk poured.

"Say when, feller."

"Uh—*when*."

The other bowl filled with creamy milk, they crumbled in corn bread, leaned elbows sociably on the bar and dined innocently and well. The night clerk waxed confidential about the hellish lonesomeness of his job from midnight on until six, when he was relieved. Camas folks crawled into their holes and pulled the hole in after them about eleven or twelve every night, he declared. Of course, if some cow outfit happened to be loading out a train of cattle, things livened up some. But it was a danged lonesome job for all that. He was glad Than happened along.

Than told his new friend who he was, where he lived and what bad luck he had suffered out on his homestead in the Broken Hills country. Burnt out, clean as a hound's tooth, he declared between mouthfuls. He'd have to start from the grass roots again. In now after a load of lumber and supplies, so he could get a roof over his head before snow flew. Soon as that was done, he'd have to haul hay from somewhere. Got a nice little start in cattle; young she stock mostly. They'd have to be fed during the worst storms. But he'd make the grade, all right.

The night clerk reached for another piece of corn bread. "That's sure hell. I was burnt out once, m'self. Say, you got a tent? Y'ain't? Well, I got a good tent I'll loan yuh the use of till you get your shack up. I'll speak to Bill, he's the day man, when he comes on at six. Er—say. You're goin' t' lay over a day, yuh say? Well, I'll have it right here in the office for yuh. Got a purty fair camp stove too, if yuh want it . . . Oh. You're buyin' a stove. Well, you take the tent an' use it long as you

127

want. 'T ain't no use to me, here in the hotel."

They ate all the corn bread, emptied the big glass pitcher of milk. Then Than turned up the lampwick, took the room key and climbed the stairs, leaving the night clerk speculatively rubbing the round bulge of his paunch.

He cast a sly, quizzically knowing glance up at Than, a glance that told of a reprehensible secret shared between them. "Say, I b'lieve you're the cause of me gittin' a belly ache," he complained. "Anybody say johnnycake an' milk, I go t' work every time an' make a dang hawg of m'self." He belched with happy repletion. "Well, g'night. Hope you ain't goin' t' suffer the way I'm liable to."

Than laughed to himself. For the next few hours, at least, his trouble with Mom would not fill his thoughts. With a sigh of contentment, he crawled between clean cool sheets and felt his weary body relax on a good spring mattress. Let tomorrow's problems wait awhile. Tonight he was fed, stretched out in comfort to sleep as long as he liked.

He blinked himself awake when the Camas school bell was ringing "last bell," however. Habit would not let him lie abed after that, so he arrived in the hotel dining room before it was quite emptied of breakfasters and ate his ham and eggs with a relish. After all, he thought, there was no sense in fooling around in Camas all that day. He wasn't a drinker, he had neither the craving nor the spare cash for gambling, and winter was coming closer every day.

Though he did not stop to analyze his change of mood, last night seemed far away. What had sent him away from the ranch, feeling as though his own family had thrust him out, had suddenly become simplified in his mind. Dade was Dade, no different than usual. Mom was feeling her oats, now that she had given Bearnson a licking. Kind of riding her high horse. She'd get over it. And on the whole, Than was not sorry that he would have a chance to build as he pleased and where he pleased and go and come without Mom's everlasting bossing. Dade was her pet, anyway. Let her stay with him if she wanted to. Than had discovered that he didn't care in the least.

Credit was easy. What cash he had in his pocket he could save for emergencies, at least, so far as Camas was concerned. By early afternoon his wagon was loaded with lumber, a plain cookstove with a large fire box that would heat his cabin, boxes of supplies, clothing, a few cooking utensils, blankets (he'd build a bunk against the wall and fill it with hay for the present). He would have to make another trip in, he saw at once. His team could not pull all he needed in one load. (Lucky Mom and Dade stocked up for winter, two full loads of stuff; they wouldn't need anything more, except lumber for Mom's room and a little furniture; let them do the worrying about that.)

While he roped his load with new rope that was stiff and inclined to kink, he whistled softly under his breath. At the moment he was able to recapture some of the thrill of his first adventuring into the country. History, he thought whimsically, was repeating itself—with certain revised chapters that ought to make better reading. Starting afresh this way, he'd know better what he wanted. And the glamorous idea of freedom to do as he pleased with his land and his life gave the future an attraction not unlike the lure of the unknown. His brain busied itself with plans. Being burnt out, he now felt, was not the unmitigated disaster it had seemed at first.

129

As he flung the new rope for the last time over the bale of hay on top of the load and leaned backward, pulling the rope tight before taking his half hitches around a brace, a harsh familiar voice made him turn, slackening the rope.

Bearnson, standing just behind him on the sidewalk, spoke again with grim irony. "You certainly made damned good time getting in."

Than stared at him blandly. "Good time doing what?"

"Good time getting in here with that team and wagon, after setting fire to a corral full of my hay! Don't try to play off innocent with me, you young whelp!"

CHAPTER SIXTEEN

THAN'S HEART SEEMED TO TURN OVER IN HIS CHEST. Tepee haystacks burned in the night! Was it possible that Mom and Dade could be guilty of a thing like that? Mom had achieved her triumph, he thought. Still, if she meant to carry on Injun warfare with Bearnson—

"What time did they burn?" He stepped up on the sidewalk and faced Bearnson. "I left right after supper. There was no fire as long as I was coming along the other side of Buffalo Butte, or I'd have seen it."

"You'd better be able to prove what time you got into town, young man. The rest of your folks have an alibi—unless King and Hoskins are both liars. They swear no one stirred from the place between dark and midnight." Bearnson watched him hard-eyed. "By your own story that doesn't cover your movements, though."

"No, it don't. They don't have to account for my time."

"Somebody better account for it, damn quick, or

you'll find yourself behind the bars. Burning other folk's hay is liable to land you in Deer Lodge, I suppose you know."

"Not a darn bit quicker than it will you, Mr. Bearnson. I don't know where you got any license to commit arson and get away with it, any more than I have."

"I didn't burn you out." Bearson brushed the charge aside with an impatient gesture of his hand. "I suppose this was your idea of getting back at me."

"I don't know what you're talking about." Than finished tying his load. "If your hay's been burned, I had nothing to do with it. I can tell you that, right now."

"Words," said Bearnson, "seem to be getting mighty cheap around here lately. It seems damn queer that the hay nearest to your place should burn last night—*inside the fireguard*—and none of you nesters know anything about it."

"Strange but true," Than observed dryly, his thoughts scurrying round and round what facts he knew, looking for some plausible explanation. "I drove in last night. Got here around two o'clock. It's just about forty-five miles from my place to Camas. Figure it out yourself."

"It's up to you to do the figuring right now. You'll have to prove what time you got into town or I'll wire in for the sheriff."

"Go ahead!" Than stepped up on the sidewalk and faced Bearnson, stern-eyed. "Go on and get your sheriff—and make a fool of yourself! I've never been near your darned haystacks. At the time you claim they were burned, I was pulling into town here."

"You'll have to prove that."

"All right, I will. You come along with me." He climbed into the wagon and motioned Bearnson to the

131

seat beside him. Almost he was tempted to make the man walk, but after all, he had to admit the Tepee owner was justified in suspecting him.

At the livery stable, the hostler came out of the shadows within the barn, a surprised look in his eyes. "What's the matter? Forgit something? I thought you pulled out long ago."

"I am pulling out right *pronto*," said Than. "Where's that night man of yours?"

"Him? Oh-h, I expect he's home, most likely. Boards with his folks, back over there behind that little hill. Want to see him?"

Bearnson showed a gleam of interest. "You used to keep a record here of who puts up or leaves, and what time."

The man shifted his quid of tobacco, spat off to one side and nodded. "Yeah, that's right. Ever since that big hold-up we git their names an' address. Damn right. We'd 'a' had them fellers cold, if we could 'a' proved—"

"Yes. Well, let's see your record; will you?" Bearnson put a foot on the wheel and jumped down nimbly for a man nearing sixty. "We have a—er—a little bet to settle, about the time it takes to drive in."

Than's eyes widened. Bearnson was whiter than he had given him credit for being, or he was playing a deeper game than appeared on the surface. He sat passive on the high spring seat while Bearnson went into the office with the stableman. When he came out, looking thoughtful, Than released the brake and took the slack out of the lines. His mouth relaxed into a sour kind of grin.

"Better get in and ride, Mr. Bearnson. I've got another way of proving you're wrong."

"You can't have too many," Bearnson retorted,

132

climbing in again. "The stable book shows you put up your team and saddle horse at one forty-five. But that doesn't explain why you brought that extra horse along, when you apparently came for a load of supplies."

"Just what are you driving at, Mr. Bearnson?"

Bearnson turned his head and stared hard at Than's unreadable profile.

"I'm wondering," he said, "what was to prevent you from leaving the team somewhere outside of town and riding back on the short cut to burn those stacks. That," he added grimly, "would have been one way of establishing an alibi."

Than snorted. "Pretty near as foxy as choosing the day when your outfit was loading out a train of cattle, and slippin' a man over west of my line to start that prairie fire, so the wind would carry it straight down across our land!"

"You haven't the faintest shadow of proof of that."

"Well, neither have you that I ducked back and set your hay afire."

"I have the fact that you brought an extra saddle horse along last night."

"Yeah!" Than draw a deep, angry breath. "And do you know why? 'Cause I didn't have hay to feed him at home. You see them three bales, back there? When they're unloaded at my camp, they'll be every spear of hay I've got on my ranch. That's why I brought my horse along; to let him fill his belly here in town. And," he added fiercely, "to make darn sure he was safe while I made this trip."

He pulled up at the Camas House, wound the lines around the brake lever and sprang out. "You want to come in and talk to the night clerk? He'll tell you when I registered, last night."

Bearnson was getting out. He did not reply until he was standing on the sidewalk again.

"I can see no advantage in talking to the night clerk," he declined then. "You've established an alibi, I can see that without going any farther." He glanced up and down the street, then back at Than with a look as keen and as cold as slivers of ice.

"Until I find some one who saw you riding that black horse last night along the short cut to my place," he said, "or who can tell me where you left this team last night, I'll have to let that alibi keep you out of jail."

"That sure is fine and accommodating of you, Mr. Bearnson! Me, I've got to wait a while too, before I can cinch that prairie fire onto you. I've got a little job ahead of me too. I've got to find out who it was traveled that big gully across your field and out to the hills where that fire of ours was started."

"What's that? Do you mean to insinuate—"

"Now, now, ain't insinuating a damn thing, Mr. Bearnson. I'm just telling yuh. When I find out who rode that gully—"

"Nobody rode that gully. Not that day, at least. My men were all here in town."

"Establishing an alibi for you!" Than grinned exasperatingly. "You know and I know that tracks don't make themselves. Now, do they? Tracks were laid the length of that gully, the day of the fire, and they were going to the hills and back again. And more than all that, a man was seen duckin' into the gully, coming from the hills just before the fire broke out. And sooner or later, I'm going to find out who that man was. So put that in your pipe and smoke on it, Mr. Bearnson."

"Trying to throw dust in my eyes, are you? Trying to raise another issue. But I warn you, young man, I'll

134

break this alibi of yours and have you behind the bars for burning my hay. And if not for that, for the next dirty work you do. Forewarned is forearmed. I know now the kind of tricks you're capable of. You're smart, but one of these days you'll be a little bit too smart. You'll make a bobble with your alibis. And I'll be right on hand with a warrant when you do. Remember that."

"Better have the sheriff bring a couple; I might be able to show him where he can use another one!"

"You sneaking, hay-burning—!"

For the name Bearnson called him, Than lashed out with his fist and landed it neatly on Bearnson's nose. Stocky, grizzled, inclined to portliness though he was, Bearnson came back with a surprising swiftness. Than ducked, felt his hat spinning off his head, got a blow on the chin that jarred him to his toes.

For the first time Bearnson began to smile, drawing his close-cropped mustache back away from his teeth, revealing unsuspected fillings of gold. It was evident that somewhere in his past he had picked up a good knowledge of boxing. And it was also apparent that he was glad of the chance to lay aside his dignity and get down to fundamentals.

Than was not much given to fighting. Since the furious battle he and Dilly had indulged in at their first meeting, he had not had cause to lift his fists to any man. Back somewhere in the dim recesses of his mind he was aware of the shame of striking a man old enough to have been his father, and the spectacle they two were making of themselves there on the most conspicuous corner in Camas.

A short-arm jab sent him reeling against a man in the circle miraculously formed around them. He came back to meet another terrific punch. He was being whipped, neatly and without delay. The thought stung him into action. Old man be damned. Bearnson didn't need any young man's pity.

Than shook his head to clear it and rushed in, fighting furiously. He felt his fist land on the cushion of flesh around one of those bleak gray eyes and gave a satisfied grunt. He saw Bearnson's smile go crooked and bloody from a blow that loosened one of those gold-filled teeth. Then some one grabbed him from behind, yanked him backward, gripping his elbows. Men closed in around Bearnson. Than fought to free himself, walking backward lest they pull him off his feet. He was around the corner, swearing because they would not let him go and finish the fight.

"Shut up, you damn' fool," Dilly hissed in his ear. "Didn't you see that tin star coming down the street? One more pass at the old man and you'd find yourself in the cooler."

"Did you hear what he called me?"

"Yeah; and I heard what you called him. It's a stand-off, if you ask me."

"You let me go. I don't care if there's forty constables on the job—"

"Hell, Than, don't you know the boss used to fight for *money?* Syd, you go drive his team on down the street. We'll meet you down there by the blacksmith shop." Dilly reached out and took Than's hat from little Rosy, set it aslant on Than's head. "Come on, old-timer. School's out for today. You closed an eye for him and made him swallow an eighteen-carat tooth; that oughta be about enough for once."

They hustled him along the alley, Than protesting every step of the way, and ventured out upon the main street only when the blacksmith shop bulked between

136

them and the little knot of men up beside the hotel. Syd Hunt was waiting with the team, Hawk standing docilely beside the mare called Nellie. Syd got down and handed the lines to Than.

"Here you are—and if there's anything else we can do for yuh, Than, why let us know. And, say! While I think of it, tell Mom she sure knows how to pop a quirt. She oughta be a mule skinner—you tell her I said she's worth a regiment of soldiers. Only time I ever seen the old man back down from a scrap."

"Yeah. Talk about whippin' her weight in wildcats—!" Rosy laughed louder than was necessary, just to complete the diversion.

With his foot on the hub, Than looked from one to the other. "All right, boys. I sabe," he said tersely. "I guess you've got the right idea, at that. Much obliged." On the seat, he leaned toward them, his foot on the brake, ready to release it and move off. "But you tell that—boss of yours, the last card ain't turned yet, by a long shot!"

CHAPTER SEVENTEEN

ANOTHER LOAD OF STRAIGHT LUMBER, GRAIN AND HAY gave Than a short respite from hauling and the time to build shelters for his horses and himself. Because he had waited only long enough to rest his horses and snatch a few hours of sleep before starting off to Camas for his second load, he saw no one from home until the third day after his quarrel with Mom. Then Susan and Blaney rode up to his camp just as he had finished laying the foundation for his stable.

"Oh, what are you doing, Than?" Susan immediately wanted to know, staring down from her pony's back.

"Me? Why, I'm tending my own business, like a good boy who always minds his mother," Than replied in his pleasantest tone, with an eyelid lowered to let Blaney know his sweetheart was merely being teased a little.

"Oh. Well, that's nice. I wondered if you really were doing it." Susan's voice was pert but her smile was uncertain. "Oh, is that your tent over there under the tree?"

"Nope," Than responded cheerfully, squinting along a two-by-four to see how straight it might be. "Good glory! I oughta take all this dimension stuff back and wrap it around that fellow's neck! About one out of every three of these two-by-fours is crooked as a ram's horn."

"Oughta watch those guys," Blaney observed with careful sympathy.

"Yeah, but I had too much running around to do, getting my stuff together. I just drove up to the lumber yard and left the team standing while I went over to the hardware store to rustle some tools."

"Dade's got hammers and saws and things," Susan volunteered, as if that was news.

"Yeah, so have I." Than picked up his new hammer with something of a flourish.

"You didn't have to go and buy tools and you know it. You just did that to show off. Who does own that tent if you don't?"

"Hunh? Oh. William Wendt."

Susan's mouth puckered in at the corners. "I don't know any William. Where'd he go? Anyway, that isn't what I asked you."

Than was busy spiking the two-by-four to his sill and he did not answer. Susan tossed her head and reined over closer to Blaney.

"Well, I brought up a loaf of fresh bread; but I may as well take it back, I guess, if this is the way you're going to act."

While he reached for another spike, Than looked up at her. "This is the way I'm going to act till I get a roof over the horses and one for myself," he said, his fine hazel eyes looking almost green in the sunlight. He glanced quickly from Susan to Blaney, who was regarding him thoughtfully. "Sorry I can't stop work and entertain you folks, but I'm afraid this good weather won't last."

"I'll go back and get Dade's tools and help you," Blaney said abruptly, passing over Than's mild sarcasm. "We didn't know whether you were here or where the deuce you were. Thought we'd ride up and see if we could get a line on you."

"Why didn't you come home like a reasonable being?" Susan demanded.

"Maybe because I'm not one."

"Mommie's all over her mad now. That—what you did to the Tepee just tickled her to pieces."

Than held his hammer suspended on a level with his skinned face while he looked at her. "Yeah? How'd you hear about that?"

"How'd we *hear?* Why, they thought maybe Dade did it! Hobe Cheever and Jim Dodson came over the very next morning, and they were right on the warpath too. Weren't they, Blaney? They just talked awful, till Mom went outside and started giving them a piece of her mind. She had it all according to the Scriptures, 'an eye for an eye and a tooth for a tooth'; only in these days, she said, it's come down to haystacks for haystacks. So then Blaney convinced them we didn't know anything about it and they went on home."

139

That, of course, was Sue's version of the affair, Than told himself, while he went on working. When Blaney repeated that he would be back to help with the stable, Than merely nodded and continued his hammering. So Mom called it an eye for an eye, did she? That was about the way she'd look at it, of course. But it gave him a heavy feeling in his chest to think Mom would egg Dade on to destroy property and let Blaney lie him out of the consequences.

Susan had a parting shot for Than. She untied the sack at her saddle horn, lowered it to the lumber pile and wheeled toward him, pivoting her pony on his hind feet in the showy way she had before Blaney.

"Well, there's your bread, you old crank. And Mommie says for you to come on home to your meals if you're through pouting, but she won't have you sit at her table looking like a thundercloud. There. That's exactly what she said. Wasn't it, Blaney?"

"You tell Mom she raised me to be a pretty good cook," Than retorted.

"I'll tell her you're still sulking. And you needn't think you're hurting any one but yourself. It certainly doesn't bother *me* any! You're just one less to wash dishes after, that's all." She gave Blaney a quick glance, as if she feared his displeasure. "I don't care!" she defended herself petulantly. "You'd be sick and tired of it too, if you'd been around Than these last few months. Whatever's got into him, I don't know, but he's been going around like a bear with a sore head. I suppose," she finished, as a last shrewd thrust, "it's because Frank cut him out with Jean!"

Than was carefully measuring lumber with his shiny new square. He neither looked up nor gave any sign that he heard, but Blaney saw his left ear turn a deep red (which seemed to prove that Sue had cannily reached to a tender spot), and took pity.

"Come on, Susan Mariar. You promised to make five hundred ginger cookies for me today, remember."

They rode away. Than worked furiously after that, wondering what imp of Satan ever put that notion into Sue's head. Now she'd blat it all over the country that he was in love with Jean MacHardie and had been turned down for Frank Hoskins. Darn sisters, anyway. So they took it for granted, did they, that he—but no, they couldn't, when they'd done it themselves. But no doubt the rest of the country thought he'd fired those stacks of Bearnson's and he supposed they'd all be chewing the rag about his fight, soon as the word got out. Maybe the Tepee boys would keep their mouths shut about it. It wouldn't help them a darned bit with the boss if they let that out; then, unless Dade or Frank Hoskins went to town, the folks might not get to know about it till things had kinda died down in Camas. In a week or so the news would be stale in town. They were always having ructions of some kind over there; that's why they had a constable.

Blaney came after a while with hammer and saw and together they got the frame of the stable up and braced and two sides sheathed.

"I don't trust this balmy weather," Than declared. "Me, I can make out all right with the tent, even if we do get a storm or two; but my horses have got to be taken care of—the way I'll have to work 'em from now on."

Blaney agreed and they hurried the boards onto the north and west sides. For the first time in years they worked together without talking of anything save the task in hand. Every subject, it seemed to Blaney, was a

141

sore subject; and Than's face did not invite conversation. There were certain small bruises and abrasions on cheek and chin which Blaney would have liked to hear explained, but he would not ask questions. And that, perhaps, was the reason for their long friendship; or one of the reasons.

They knocked off at noon and Than warmed up the coffee and set out a lunch of baker's bread, bologna and canned peaches. "Got to save all the time I can from cooking," he explained briefly, and Blaney had the rare tact to refrain from mentioning the excellent cooking down the creek. Instead, he praised the bread and declared that folks could say what they liked, he could eat bologna sausage day in and day out without any trouble at all.

At sunset the chill of frost was in the air. Blaney gathered his tools together and tucked them under the diminishing pile of lumber.

"You better come on down to supper, Than," he said, with just the right shade of urgency in his tone.

"No—I've got some things in camp I want to do. Thanks just the same, Blaney."

Blaney hesitated. "The Robertses stand together, I thought."

"Sure, they do. But we're entitled to a difference of opinion amongst ourselves, just the same."

"Your mother's sorry now she talked the way she did."

"Yeah; well, that's all right. I've got a lot to do up here. And I kinda like baching, to tell you the truth, Blaney. It's kinda crowded down there, anyway."

"I've been sleeping with Dade," Blaney explained. "Sue and Mom seem to lean on me a good deal since you left. But if you want me up here to help—"

142

"You're doing a lot more, staying down there. Dade spends too much time riding around. Big cattleman," Than grinned ironically. "All of a hundred head of cattle to ride herd on."

Blaney nodded understandingly. "He'll never buckle right down to hard work, if he can get out of it. You know, I don't like that cough he's got. Maybe he's not able—"

"You better give him a gentle hint about hauling in his hay before a storm hits us. He can't expect me to do it all. And that extra room ought to be built on right away too."

"I'll look after that myself. Well, if you won't come down for supper, I'll be drifting."

While he fed and watered the horses, filled the wagon box with hay and tied them so they could eat in comfort, Than watched rather lonesomely Blaney's receding figure. But even while he watched, his mouth was set in stubborn lines that had no thought of yielding. Blaney was filling his place in the family a lot better than he ever had. It was time he broke away from Mom's apron strings and lived his own life, anyhow. She didn't need him any longer.

While he cooked his solitary supper, washed his plate and cup, his knife and fork and spoon, Than whistled resolutely over the brief task. Afterwards, with a new pencil and a new tablet of unruled paper, he drew a plan of the house he meant to build next year. This shack he was about to build would be the lean-to woodshed later on. He'd make it big enough to store a winter's supply––a fireplace sure ate up the wood! Worth it, though. He wouldn't have a house without a fireplace. He decided that he would build it on the south end of the house, and have a window each side and settees beneath; rustic;

143

made of split logs, maybe, to match the split-log mantel.

Windows to the south. You bet. Winter nights when the moon was full, it would be great to sit there beside the fire and look out over the valley . . .

By that mysterious alchemy of the imagination, a picture took form there in that weather-stained tent on the knoll. Clear as life before his mental vision he saw a room—or, more accurately, the south end of a room—with a fireplace and two windows, one on each side. The fire had died to a heap of glowing embers but the room was snug and warm. The floor was not carpeted. It was dark and shining and almost completely covered with rugs, and there were books and magazines scattered about; *Century, Harpers, McClure's* (Dade wasn't the only one in the family who liked to read; he was merely the only one who took the time).

Outside, the night was crackling cold. The stars were big as apples, sparkling like polished gold. The moon rode high, one side warped a little with age, but serene and shining. A white flake of cloud drifted slowly up across the lower part, giving the man in the moon a comical effect of long white whiskers like Santa Claus. They laughed a little over that and then were quiet again, looking out into the brilliant, cold night.

They! (Than's breath caught in his throat.) She was there, curled up on the settee beside him, snuggled within the crook of his arm. When she stirred, a black wave of her hair stole up and kissed his mouth. And she laughed that teasing little laugh of hers and said, "Weel, weel, 'tis a braw bricht nicht the noo, laddie!" And to punish her for that, he slipped a hand beneath her chin, tilted her face up and held it so while he kissed—while he kissed—

A coyote, smelling bacon rinds, yapped shrilly just

144

down beyond the big pine tree. Than jumped, blinked his eyes as if he had been startled from sleep. He caught up his new rifle, threw up the flap of the tent and stood there peering. When the coyote impudently repeated his querulous plaint, Than fired three shots for answer. He waited, but the night was still.

He went back inside, picked up the house plan he had drawn, wadded it savagely between his two palms and lifted a stove lid, poking the paper down between two half-burned sticks and standing there watching with fierce eyes until it had burned to ashes.

So do our dreams betray our most jealously guarded secrets.

When Blaney passed by on the road next morning with Dade's team and wagon, bound for town and the lumber for Mom's room, Than was sheathing the stable and whistling "Georgia Campmeeting," his hammer merrily trying to keep up with the tune.

"Anything you want in town?" Blaney shouted, slowing the team to a walk.

"Yeah!" Than shouted back. "Bring me ten pounds of ten-penny nails! And say! See if you can dig up some magazines!"

Blaney nodded, waved his hand and drove on up the road. Than went back to his hammering and his whistling and found a real pleasure in both.

CHAPTER EIGHTEEN

OF COURSE IT WAS THAN'S OWN FAULT THAT HE WAS left to himself after that. He knew it. Susan was not the kind to overlook a rebuff, nor were Mom and Dade. He was well aware that Sue's natural inclination to make the most of any story she told would color his message to Mom and make it plain that he wanted to be left alone. And that was true, up to a certain point. They were carrying it considerably further than he had bargained for, however. In the next week not a soul came near him except Blaney, and he came after Dade's carpenter tools and to bring the nails and magazines. He was going to build the addition to Dade's cabin himself, he said. There wasn't room to turn around, the way things were. It was getting on Susie's nerves.

Than grinned to himself after Blaney was gone. Henpecked already, he told himself ironically. Blaney engaged to Sis was a Blaney tamed, meekly ordering his life to please a spoiled young woman who had been babied all her life and would always demand more than she gave. It began to look as though he and Blaney were being deliberately kept apart; to bring him to time, Than suspected. But he was one member of the family Sis had never been able to drive; it was rather late in the day for her to expect him to eat out of her hand. Let her go on calling him sulky. It didn't hurt anything, so far as Than could see.

As a matter of fact, he was too busy, these days, to miss any of them very much. He had finished the stable, even to the stalls and mangers, and had hauled down a load of poles from the hills and made a small corral for temporary use. Now he was hurrying to finish his cabin before the fine weather broke. He might even get a few loads of hay hauled before it stormed. After expecting each morning for ten days to see storm clouds pushing up over the skyline, Than had turned optimist. Northern Montana did have those long balmy spells late in the fall, some years. This seemed to be one of them. Give him another week or two and he'd be ready to face anything that came along.

He was not whistling at this particular time. He had been fitting a window frame and had pinched a finger rather badly. He was damning things generally when Jean MacHardie put her head in at the opening and made round eyes at him, her two hands over her ears.

"Hoot, mon!" she cried in a shocked tone.

"I'm hooting," Than told her wickedly. And suddenly the pain was gone, forgotten. "Walk in," he invited, waving a hand toward the blank doorway. "You're my first caller. Have a seat?"

He picked up a board and laid it across a nail keg nearly empty, took her hand with mock gallantry and bowed her to the seat.

"'Tis a braw wee hoose, laddie," Jean praised it politely, gazing around with exaggerated admiration.

"It'll be a darn sight brawer when I get it floored and ready to live in." Leaning against the wall with his feet crossed, unconsciously making a picture of a thoroughly contented young man, Than pulled out tobacco sack and papers and proceeded to make a cigarette.

"Mon, ye should hae floored it while ye had free room tae swing your boards," Jean criticized. "Noo there'll be the windae and the door and the walls tae interfere—ye'll bash oot yer windae with a board; mind what I tell ye!"

Than chuckled. "Bagpipes are squealing today, I see. What's on your mind?"

"A wee bit hair and my hat. Lad, did ye no get a black eye from yon Bearnson?"

Than gave her a quick, surprised look, the rolled cigarette poised halfway to his lips. "So that's it. How'd you hear?"

Jean smiled with her eyes in the way that always

made Than feel slightly dizzy and confused. "It's true, then. I didna believe it altogether."

"How'd you come to hear of it? From Sis? I didn't want the folks to find it out."

Jean shook her head, still with that shining, smiling look in her eyes. "I doubt if they've heard it at all. Susan would have told me."

"Bet your life she would. Sis never passes up the chance to tell all she knows and then some."

"Tut-tut, lad." But her look was not reproving. "No, it was Frank told me. He had it from some of the Tepee boys who pulled you off the old man."

"Old man, my foot! He was handing it to me right and left and looking like he was having the time of his life."

"'Twas ill work, carrying the fight to Bearnson," said Jean, wrapping a shaving curl round and round her gloved finger. "He's a hard man to cross, I'm thinking."

Cigarette lighted, Than tossed the match out through the window opening and slid down upon his boot heels. Abstractedly he picked up another shaving curl, mate to Jean's, and held it dangling from thumb and finger while he smoked and watched her.

"I didn't carry the fight to Bearnson, as it happens," he said, frowning a little that she should think him a trouble hunter. "I was getting ready to pull out with my load when he came along and tore into me about burning his haystacks. Good glory! I'd made a night drive into town and I didn't even know his darned stacks had burned. He—"

"You didn't—*know?*" The shaving sprang open and fell to the floor as Jean released it. "Frank—every one thinks you did it."

Than's lip curled. "Frank—and everybody—has got

148

another think coming, then." But immediately he looked sorry he had said that. "Don't pass that on, will you, Jean?"

Their eyes met, held for two long breaths then moved away leaving a heightened color in Jean's face, a paleness in Than's.

"You know I won't—if you'd rather I didn't."

"Let them think what they please. They will, anyway. I suppose," Than added, with some bitterness, "folks take it for granted that would be the logical way of getting back at them. I don't know; maybe they're right. But—I'd rather take it out of Bearnson's hide. I don't fight dumb animals."

Jean nodded assent. "The Tepee's poor cows and the calves will winter on short rations," she said. "Bearnson will never buy that much hay."

"No, he worships the almighty dollar too much." He gave a wry smile. "That's why it hurt him. It hit him where he lives—in the pocketbook."

Jean gave a little irrepressible gurgle of laughter. "And is that where you hit him, lad? In his pocketbook?"

Than's laugh held a note of chagrin. "I couldn't seem to hit him much of anywhere. Only two good licks I got in counted, though. I managed to plant them where they'd show up the most."

"Frank says the boys told him Bearnson is a sight to behold. But he took the first train out to Helena. Frank thinks—"

"Frank! Are you going to be just an echo of Frank Hoskins, now you're engaged?" Than could have bitten his tongue off for blurting that protest, but the words were out and he could not recall them.

Jean was looking at him and her eyes dazzled Than,

149

they were so shining. "And would the echo of Frank not be—"

"I'm sorry I said that, Jean. I—a man's a damn fool sometimes. Only—I guess I am all the time."

"Yes," Jean assented, almost in a whisper. "You're all of that, I'm thinking!"

Than's head went up with a jerk. His eyes bored deep into hers, until she stooped to recover her curled shaving. For a long minute she was very busy curling it around her finger just so; too busy to look up and meet the steady gaze he bent upon her face.

"What made you say that?"

"Say what?"

"You know. That about my being a—a fool all the time."

"I dinna ken—but ye said it yersel', ye mind—"Never was a shaving curled as meticulously exact as that one must be to satisfy Jean MacHardie. Abruptly the atmosphere within that smelly, tar-papered shack had become electric. Jean sat there as if she never meant to move again and the loosely knotted white neckerchief she wore palpitated noticeably with her quick breathing.

"Jean!"

Jean's hands shook. She did not look up or make a sound, though her lips moved.

"Jean, why am I a fool all the time?"

Jean gave a nervous little laugh. "It could be —you—"

"I'm what?"

"A—a blind fool, maybe. I dinna ken."

Than breathed as though he had just come in from a run uphill. His eyes never left her face; searching, probing, hungering. The silence tightened.

"You do know. You know you—and Frank are—"

"We're not!" There was pain in Jean's voice and a

frantic appeal. She gave him one swift look and let her lashes fall close to her cheek again.

"You're —not—"

"No! He—asked me so many times and I then at last I was in a mood—I telt him to gie me six months to make up my mind—"

Than waited, watched her, held his breath, fearing what might come next. "Well?" His voice was harsh with strain. "And did you?"

"Yes." Jean's face was white.

Again that silence. Than broke it with something like a groan. "A blind fool. You're dead right. I might have had a chance—and I was too blind to see it." He got up, turned to the high window opening, leaned against the side, plucking savagely at a break in the selvage edge of tar paper.

Abruptly he whirled upon her. "You said you're not engaged. D'you mean you told him—no?"

Jean shook her head, "He hasn't asked for his answer —yet. The six months—"

"Not up yet. I see." He laughed hardly, tossed his dead cigarette out upon the ground. "Some fellows might try and cut in ahead—"

"Not—blind men."

He was beside her, holding her tenderly by the shoulders. "Good God, Jean! Would you—? But I can't do that. Not till you've given Frank his answer. Why don't you? What are you waiting for?"

All Jean's fine poise, her teasing little tones were gone. She looked frightened. Trapped.

"I can't—until he asks for it. It was agreed that he would wait—six months—"

"Under the circumstances," Frank's voice drawled at the window, "I'll waive that agreement, Jean. You can

151

tell me now. I'm ready to take my medicine."

Absorbed in each other, held insulated within their own emotions, they had not heard him come. They started, Than stood away from her, on guard.

"I guess it's *no*, isn't it, Jean?" Frank prompted her, as if he wanted it over with quickly.

Jean nodded, gazing at him blindly through unshed tears. "I'm sorry, Frank."

"Better leave that to me," Frank said roughly. "I'll have all my life to be sorry in." He bit his lip, turned to Than. "You win. I'll admit I've been afraid you might. Sorry I interrupted this interesting little scene. Saw Jean's horse down by the corral and thought maybe she'd like company on the way home. I was mistaken."

"After eavesdropping—"

"No. You've got me wrong. These tar-paper shacks are mighty thin, remember. They leak sound like a sieve. Well, good luck to you both. Let me be the first to wish you joy."

Than sent a sidelong look toward Jean and grinned rather helplessly. "Good glory, Frank! I don't know yet whether I've got any joy coming to me. Seems to me you're kinda previous."

Frank gave him a look of pity. "Well, if you don't know, you're a bigger fool than I take you for. I could have told you months ago you had only to crook your finger. I guess I banked too hard on your not getting wise to yourself. Well, so long, folks. I—hope you'll be happy, Jean."

Jean was sitting very still with her hands tightly clasped in her lap. She looked at Frank, the tears slipping down her cheeks.

"You're a better mon than I thought ye, Frank. You'll find a girl that loves ye—and I hope you'll be

152

verra happy."

Frank waved a hand and was gone. In a moment Than looked and saw him riding away, spurring his horse, jerking him as if he were trying to break an outlaw's stubbornness.

Than's eyebrows pulled together. His eyes were puzzled. Then they cleared. That was not the real Frank Hoskins, he told himself. That was just a bitter mood made all the more savage because he had held himself in. Acted like a gentleman, Frank had. You couldn't blame him for fighting his horse just to relieve his feelings.

He turned away from the window, lifted Jean up into his arms and held her close.

"Y-ye'll be thinking me a bold baggage, laddie," Jean whispered, when her lips were free.

"Bold? And here I've been eating my heart out—and almost lost you!"

Jean laughed, hid her face against his shoulder.

"What are you laughing at now? I did lose you, almost."

"Oh, ay," said Jean in her best Scotch accent; "'tis the blind that maun hae the wee bit guidance, ye onderstand !"

"Bagpipes are squealing," Than announced the second time since she came. "I knew something was on your mind, lassie."

"'Tis naught save a braw lad who sh'd be pittin' thae windae in his wee bit hoose." She broke from him, abandoning her accent with the bewildering abruptness that was her habit. "Pick up your hammer, or whatever you use for the work, and fit the window while I hold it. Fine days won't last much longer, lad, and I'll be far easier in my mind when I know you've a snug cabin when the first big blizzard strikes."

153

That was Jean. Practical, efficient, thinking first of all of her man's comfort and well being.

Than grinned appreciatively, picked up his tools and went to work.

CHAPTER NINETEEN

WITH HIS SOUR-DOUGH COAT BUTTONED TO HIS CHIN and with a silk neckerchief tied over his ears under his big gray Stetson, Dilly let himself through Than's west gate, closed it after him, and rode north along the fence to the timber along Running Man. There, keeping well under cover, he rode down the creek, leaving the brush just behind Than's cabin.

He pulled up there and eyed the stovepipe from which a mere wisp of smoke rose thinly, almost invisible unless one were close and watched for it. Dilly studied it, glancing up toward the sun which was no more than a lighter blur in the close-packed gray clouds hurrying eastward before the biting west wind that was purpling his cheeks and his nose; looked down toward the low tar-papered stable and saw a forkful of litter thrown out of the small window facing the shack. With a grunt he twitched the reins and rode on down there.

"Oh, Than!" he called sharply, as he neared the stable door. "Come on out here a minute, will yuh?"

Pitchfork still in his hand, Than appeared in the doorway. "Oh, hello, Dilly," he greeted, with some surprise. "Get down and lead your horse in here outa that wind. It's enough to singe the hair off a polar bear."

"Can't stop more'n two seconds—hardly that long," Dilly explained. But he dismounted, nevertheless, and came leading his horse into the grateful warmth of the stable. "Sure is cold today but I've got to be drifting in a minute. I ain't supposed to be up this way, nohow."

Something of tense significance in his tone made Than look at him sharply with an indefinable sense of catastrophe.

"What's the matter, Dilly? Anything happened?"

Dilly gave him a fleeting glance and looked away again. "I kinda thought you ought to know that—well, the Old Man has got next," he said shamefacedly, as if he were confessing some fault of his own. "He's sure going to raise Cain. I just thought I'd better ride over and give yuh the tip."

Than stared. "Going to raise Cain, is he? What about?"

Dilly pulled off his gloves, stuffed them into his pocket and reached for his makings. His fingers seemed all thumbs. It seemed as though he never would get one cigarette paper separated from the others in the little orange-colored book. His face was more troubled than ever Than had seen it.

"If Bearnson goes to raising Cain, I'm liable to be right there to help with the raising," Than said.

"You—I don't believe you get me, Than. It's about them Pothooks. Six head uh cows with their calves. We'd about finished rounding up the calves to wean 'em, when these damned critters come ambling outa the brush like they'd been drove out. That was back up here in the hills." Dilly tilted his head toward the west. "I don't believe anybody noticed anything about 'em till we started working the bunch yesterday at the ranch. Even then," he explained carefully, "it was afternoon before the Old Man spotted one uh the cows and got wise. So—" He hunched his shoulders expressively.

"Well, what about it, Dilly? What are you driving at,

anyway?"

Dilly lifted the tiny paper roll to his lips, moistened its edge while he eyed Than curiously. "Maybe I didn't make myself plain as I oughta done," he said dryly. "What I meant is this: They was Pothooks a month or so ago; maybe less. The brands ain't scabbed off yet. They *was* Pothooks. Now they're Cross N's."

While he found a match, struck it sharply along the wall, lighted his cigarette and took three leisurely puffs, there was no sound save the whooing of the wind whistling around the stable.

Than drew a long careful breath. "They were Pothooks; now they're Cross N's," he repeated, as if he were memorizing the statement. His fingers clenched into a fist, then relaxed and hung straight along the pitchfork handle. "D'you mind showing me how it was done, Dilly?" Dilly gave him a quick incredulous glance. "You want it drawed out for yuh?" He seemed not to believe his ears.

"Yeah. If you don't mind."

"Simple—so darned simple it's a wonder to me the boss has got any Pothooks left at all." He searched with his eyes for something that would make a mark, found a tough bit of wild sunflower stalk almost at his feet, picked it up and stooped to draw a symbol on the earthen floor of the stable.

$$\left|\!\!\!/\right.$$

"There's the Pothook," he remarked. "Easiest brand in the world to work. That's what they used to be."

Then, with the sunflower stalk threatening to break

under the pressure, he drew another brand.

"And there," he added ironically, "is what them Pothook cows and calves claim to be now. Your Cross N."

He stood up and looked strangely at Than. "It was a pretty good job of altering," he said, in a flat colorless tone. "If they'd of had time to hair over, the devil himself couldn't have told the difference without skinnin' the critter and lookin' on the wrong side of the hide. But they're too raw yet. And there's one old cow that any man in the outfit could swear to on a stack uh Bibles as high as your head."

Than was staring hard at the telltale marks on the stable floor. He did not look up or answer, though Dilly waited until his cigarette was smoked down to a stub. He pinched out the fire in it, threw it out into the hard-packed snow from the storm three days before. His glance went searching Than's face.

"I couldn't stand by and see the stock inspector or the sheriff ride up here and you not looking for him," he said. "The Old Man told us all to keep our traps shut or we could roll our blankets and drift; and this is a damn poor time uh year to get let out of a job, Than. You know that. But I rode the gully through to the fence and followed that down to the brush. I just *had* to put you wise. And if there's anything else I can do, let's hear it."

Than lifted his head and looked Dilly full in the eyes. "There's just one thing—but it ain't likely you can do it."

"Name it and I'll sure do it."

"I wish you could take my word for it that I don't know the first damn thing about how those Pothooks got worked over into our brand. All I know is, I didn't do it."

He watched Dilly's face, met the long, keen probing of Dilly's eyes. When Dilly's glance swung away and began studying a broken board in the stall partition just before him, Than's heart went heavy. Of course, he couldn't expect any one to believe him. The evidence was damning.

"It ain't what I think that counts," Dilly said worriedly, at last. "It's what shows on them cattle. And everybody in the country knows you've had it in for Bearnson. Them burnt haystacks 'll likely be drug into the case."

"But I—"

"Don't make no difference what you done or didn't do," Dilly talked down Than's voice of protest. "You'll get the name of it, anyhow. And nobody but a damn fool would wait till the sheriff rides up and serves a warrant on yuh for rustling. Which will be tomorrow, most likely." From sheer nervousness he began to make himself another cigarette. He lighted it, blew out the match, tossed the charred stick outside. "Ain't there something I can do, Than?"

Than shook his head. He was still staring at the crude markings at his feet and his fingers were gripping the pitchfork handle until their knuckles were white.

"The Old Man went in this morning to catch the noon train for Chinook," Dilly said, picking up the bridle reins and moving toward the door, pulling his horse after him. "He aims to bring the inspector—or else the sheriff—back with him tomorrow. He didn't say so, but that's the way we've got it sized up at the ranch."

"I see."

"If you're shy on money, Than, I've got twenty dollars in my jeans that you can have and welcome. I just about got cleaned in a poker game the other night in town, or I'd have more," he explained apologetically. "You better take this, anyway."

Than's eyes softened. "No, you keep it, Dilly. I'm not broke yet. I'll get along."

"The Old Man'll never quit now till you're all flat, stony broke," Dilly exclaimed bitterly. "He don't know when to quit, once he gets started. And he's been laying for you ever since that scrap in town."

"Yeah, I expect he has, all right."

Dilly gathered up the reins, lifted his bulky overshoed foot to the stirrup. In the saddle he turned for a last word.

"You take my advice, Than. Don't ever let this thing get into court, if you can help it. Keep a jump or two ahead of 'em. I tell yuh straight. It means the pen, sure, for one of yuh—if not both."

"All right, Dilly." Than could not have told next minute what words he spoke. His thoughts reeled dizzily, sent spinning by Dilly's last sentence. The pen for both. *Both!*

There was no need for Dilly to linger. There was nothing more to be said, no more that he could do. Yet he seemed reluctant to ride away. He held his horse in with so tight a rein it backed and sidled, tail whipping between its legs in the wind.

"Don't hit for the Line, whatever you do!" he cried a last warning. "Them mounted police are hell hounds."

"Thanks. I won't, Dilly."

"Well—be good to yourself! I gotta be drifting—"

"So long, Dilly. Thanks for the tip."

159

From the doorway Than watched him go galloping up past the cabin and into the woods beyond. When there was neither sight nor sound of him, Than turned mechanically back to his work, piling the mangers with hay. "They were Pothooks. They ain't now; they're Cross N's." His mind kept repeating Dilly's words over and over, now and then adding that other sentence for good measure. "It means the pen sure, for one if not both." Underneath the words ran a full swift current of thoughts, plans, conjectures. Mom and Sis and Blaney. Dade—he tried to keep Dade out of it, but without success. "The damned fool!" he muttered once. But immediately Dade was back in his mind. Dade with his finicky ways—"a pretty good job—" Dade with his cough "—the pen sure for one if not for both." Whatever had possessed him to do a crazy thing like that. Dade couldn't live a year, shut away from the sun—

Of Jean, too, he thought achingly. A double wedding they had meant to have with Blaney and Sis, after all. Christmas wedding. Jean railed at the idea of their waiting until he had his real house built; the one with the fireplace in the south end. If a tar-paper shack was good enough for her lad, then it was good enough for her. Or a tent would do if necessary. Just as she had fought fire with him, trying to save his home, so now she would fight beside him to build anew.

And tomorrow was Thanksgiving day. Would the sheriff leave his Thanksgiving dinner to come out and arrest the two Roberts boys? Then he wondered if it would be legal to arrest a man on a holiday. Jean and her father were coming over for dinner and Than himself had ridden to a neighbor's fifteen miles away and bought a turkey, because Mom's had perished in the fire, hiding in the brush along with the chickens.

What about tomorrow? Jean would have little appetite for turkey—no one would feel much like celebrating. And with the thought came strong desire. Whatever the future might hold, today he must see Jean. He would ride down there. He would have time—Dilly said the sheriff would not come before tomorrow. He need not tell her. Still, she'd be sure to find it out. No matter. He wouldn't spoil his last visit with her. He'd go now. There would be nothing strange in his riding over to see her today—

Hoof beats crunched outside. "Hello!" a voice called into the wind. "Anybody there?"

The sheriff! Than drew his foot sidewise across the telltale marks in the dirt. "Hello!" he answered and went to the open doorway.

Not the sheriff, after all. Big, sandy-mustached Hobe Cheever, the Tepee foreman. He pulled his horse up in the shelter of the stable and looked down at Than.

"Say, Than, I just rode over to put you next to something you'll maybe want to side-step."

"Yeah?"

"We ran onto a bunch of Pothooks yesterday that had been worked over into Cross N's. Uh course, as foreman of the Tepee, I'm a dirty double-crosser, coming and telling you about it. I wouldn't let one of the boys do it. But I'll be damned if I'll sit tight and let Bearnson nail you to the cross without giving you a chance to duck." He did not dismount, as Dilly had done. His whole attitude betrayed uneasiness and a haste to be done with a disagreeable business.

"You better pass the word to your brother, if he had any hand in it," he went on. "I don't s'pose he did. The Old Man seems to think you played a lone hand. They'll

161

be after yuh about tomorrow or next day—tomorrow bein' Thanks givin'," he added. Then, as Than showed no inclination to reply, he said impatiently,

"Damn it, man, you might have known you couldn't get away with it, so close to home. You sure took a long chance—but that's your affair, I guess. You better make tracks while you've got the chance. But don't head north. They'll pick you up across the Line, sure as hell."

"Much obliged, Hobe. Better come up to the shack and get warm."

But Hobe stated that he was in a hurry and proved it by riding at a swift gallop into the teeth of the west wind.

When he could no longer see Hobe on the trail, Than threw the saddle on Hawk and galloped down the creek. Not that he distrusted the Tepee foreman; but he did think it would be just as well if his movements from now on were not known to any of the Tepee outfit.

At Dade's place no one was in sight. For a moment he was half decided to stop and call Dade out and tell him what he had heard; ask him what fiend possessed him. But that would do no good and it would take some precious minutes. Perhaps they wouldn't bother Dade. It was himself Bearnson wanted to smash.

He loped on down the creek, on the trail he had kept well beaten, clear and distinct in spite of falling snow and shifting, wind-blown drifts. A joyous trail it had been for Than; an eager, swift trail, for it led to Jean. But today there was no joy.

"They were Pothooks. Now they're Cross N's," clacked the hoofs of his horse. "Good God!"

CHAPTER TWENTY

"I KEN FINE YOU'RE IN TROUBLE, LAD," JEAN REPEATED for the third time. "And why will ye no' tell me it?"

For the third time Than laughed at her and tried to take her in his arms. Except that his eyes were dark and troubled, he was quite convincingly gay.

Jean skillfully evaded the embrace. "If ye'll no' trust me, lad, ye'll no' kiss me," she declared with more firmness than the occasion would seem to warrant.

"Good glory! All the trouble I've got is wondering why you won't kiss me today. Mad because I didn't come yesterday?"

Jean shook her head, studying his face.

"Than, you're in trouble. I knew it when I saw you ride in the gate. I can see it in your eyes now. I hear it when you laugh. What is it?"

"Nothing but your imagination. Forget it—"

She shook her head at him. "A man can't hide trouble—not from the girl who loves him, laddie. I think you're afraid to worry me. But I'm worrying far more because you'll not trust me. I can bear trouble—I can bear *anything* but that look of tragedy in your eyes. They canna lie, laddie, no matter what the tongue says about it."

Her arms were around his neck then, and her shining eyes were reflecting his own image. They dazzled him just as they always had done. With a suppressed groan, he pressed her face down against his shoulder where he could not see those terribly blue eyes of hers.

"You're talking straight American half the time today," he parried. "I want my Scotch lassie back, that's

163

what."

Jean pulled herself free. "Well—all right. But if you want your Scotch lassie, you'll have to keep the clouds from coming between us. You'll have to trust me with your worries as well as your joys."

"I do—I shall, when I have any."

"There's something now. If—when we're married— you'll have to share your troubles—"

"Sure."

She made one further attempt. "Than, can you look me straight in the eyes and tell me there's nothing?"

Than believed that he could and he was foolish enough to try it. But he failed to take into account his deep love for her and the anguish of knowing he would not see her again, would not be able to go through with that Christmas wedding. For just about three seconds he met her clear gaze. The next he knew, his head was bowed, face buried in her hair. He was crushing her in his arms and fighting off a childish sobbing such as had not seized him for years.

They were standing near a couch. Jean pulled him to it, forced him to sit down. She sat beside him, gripped in his arms. Her voice was hushed, trembling yet intrepidly cheerful.

"The bagpipes are ae squealing a richt bonnie tune, lad. An' wull ye no' listen? Wi' them skirlin' an' pipin' before us, shall we no' climb togither?"

"Jean! Oh, Jean!"

"Trouble I can bear. I can laugh at it, Than with you. But to have you shut me outside—"

"You're right. You'll have to know sometime. It may as well—It's this. I—just heard today. There's a little bunch of six cows and calves over at the Tepee. They were Pothooks. Now they're Cross N's."

Jean was too experienced a cowgirl not to know what that meant. She did not ask any questions. She kissed the white line on his forehead where his hat had shielded it from sun and wind; and after that she stared unseeingly at the opposite wall.

"Dade, of course. What a fool he must be!"

Than held her off and looked at her strangely. "God bless you, girl! I was afraid you might think—"

"Shame on ye! Well ye should know I'd think nothing of the kind. You say you *heard*. Who told you that, Than?"

"Dilly. It would cost him his job if Bearnson found out he'd tipped me off. And Hobe Cheever came over and warned me, too."

"Hobe I might suspect was bluffing you, Than. Dilly––I couldn't think Dilly would help in a frame-up."

"He wouldn't. I'd trust him same as I do Blaney. But he thinks *I* did it, Jean. So does Hobe. He said straight out that I'm the one Bearnson's out to get. He's gone in now to swear out a warrant and they're holding the cattle for evidence. Dilly thought they might take Dade––both of us. The sheriff—or maybe the stock inspector, if he's there—will be out tomorrow, probably."

"Well," said Jean, "you must get him away before then. It would break Mom's heart if anything happened her David. He can get away, though—"

Than's free hand caressed her hair. "No, girlie. That won't do. I'm going to pull out, myself." He felt her wince and hurried on before she could protest, "Dade doesn't know the country like I do. He's never got right out and roughed it. That shack is about as close to nature as he's ever been. And with that cough of his he never could stand it. And if they took him and—sent him up—He couldn't stand that, either. Nor Mom,

165

either. So you see—"

"I do *not* see! He should have thought of these things—

"It's because he doesn't know the game that he did it. He's nothing but a tenderfoot, really; just playing at handling cattle. He'd helped me brand our calves and it looked easy—No, I'm elected, Jean. They think I'm the one that did it, just as they think I burned that corral full of hay that night. They think I'm getting back at Bearnson this way. I'm going to drift, to-night. And I want you to promise me you won't say anything—what I said about Dade. I'm the cowpuncher of the family, don't you see? If I pull out, they'll forget all about him and take in after me. And," he finished grimly, "I'll sure give them a run for their money!"

"Than, you shall not do it. I'll not let you do it. I think it's a perfectly crazy idea—"

"No, it isn't. It's the only way out. Dade's got to stay with Mom. I can get away and keep them guessing. I— I'm not enough of a martyr to go to the pen for Dade, but I'll go on the dodge for a while till this blows over. And you'll help me by—"

"I shall not help you do an insane thing like that. Dade is not the man you are; not the help to his mother. He's a selfish egotist. What if his lungs are weak? That's not your fault. There is nothing in his lungs to make him a thief and if there were—"

"But don't you see, Jean? I've *got* to go, unless I want to be railroaded to Deer Lodge. They take it for granted I worked those brands. Dilly said himself that Bearnson won't quit now till we're flat broke. I tell you, Jean. If I sign a relinquishment to my claims, will you hold them down for me till I come back? I can do it. I'll slip into Chinook before they know I'm on the dodge, relinquish

166

to you and beat it. I know Valley County like a book. There's dozens of fellows hiding out in there and I'll go there and keep outa sight till this is settled." He caught her two arms, held her off and looked at her as if he would never be able to give her up.

"It's the only way, Sweetheart. They'll send me over the road, Dade or no Dade—if they catch me. But they won't. I promise you that."

"You—you're just trying to play the hero! Well, be hero enough to let him pay the price, why don't you? He would. He'd never send his own brother to the penitentiary; he isn't that vile. He'll confess he did it and they'll have to let you go. Than! Can't you be brave enough to be just—to yourself, if not to me? You think you're doing a fine, brave thing, but you're not. You're a coward, Than Roberts. You're afraid to trust Dade to do the decent thing. But I know him better than you do. Selfish he is, full of his own importance—but he'll never let you take this upon yourself. He has his pride too."

"Not pride enough to keep his hands off another man's property," Than said bitterly.

"But that was in revenge, perhaps. But if he doesn't tell the truth, I'll pile up the evidence against him until––She broke down suddenly and wept, her head against his shoulder.

But even her tears, the first he had ever seen fall from Jean's eyes, could not alter Than's decision. All his life he had been made to see that Dade must be considered first. He had been a delicate child and Than must look after him; a spoiled child who got what he wanted and let Than take the leavings. Now, those years of petty sacrifices and shieldings made it utterly unthinkable that he should not protect Dade.

167

With Jean's tears—and his own, if the truth were known—still damp on his face, he rode away at last, not yielding an inch from his determination. He did not feel that he was doing something fine and brave. He knew only that this was something he was doing because he must.

After that talk with Jean he had no heart or courage left to face Mom and Susan. Blaney, he knew, had left before daylight for town, meaning to make the round trip in one day. He was glad of that. They would know it soon enough. Probably they would think him guilty. In the face of that damning evidence, even Blaney could believe nothing else. He felt that he would rather not see any of them again.

That afternoon he set his place in order, turned his team loose in the corral with the gate open and the stable door propped wide. There was plenty of hay in the mangers; he saw to that. Blaney or Dade would look after them.

He laid out his two heaviest blankets of Canadian wool, folded to go under his saddle. He took a canvas nosebag, put in it half a sack of oats, wrapped them in half a tarp ready to tie on his saddle when he was ready to go. He also made a small pack of salt, a few pounds of flour, half a side of bacon, some tea, a frying pan, lard bucket and a full carton of matches. To this he added his gun, four boxes of cartridges and his winter's supply of tobacco. His coffee was unground and he did not bother with it.

At dusk he rode away down the creek, steeling his mind against stopping at Dade's cabin, though a light in the window seemed to beckon. They were looking for Blaney, he supposed. The trail to MacHardie's was something to endure with what fortitude he could call to his aid. He was glad when he could turn off toward Snowbird Creek, where Frank Hoskins had his claim, and thus avoid passing the MacHardie house nearer than a mile. Frank, he thought, would not be sorry to hear the news. Perhaps he would try again for Jean's love. Well, he had certainly taken his medicine like a man, and though he had quit MacHardie and gone back to his ranch, he had not sulked nor changed his manner toward Than.

For a few minutes Than was tempted to stop in and see Frank. Lone bachelors were always glad to see some one ride in. But he decided that it would be foolish to let folks know which direction he had taken. The Canadian border was only fifty miles away. He could cross it before the turkeys would be carved tomorrow or the fiddles twanged for the Thanksgiving dances on his own side the Line. They'd look there first, of course.

But he had not needed Dilly or Hobe Cheever to warn him against the scarlet-coated riders who patroled the hills and coulees across the border. Nor was he so simple as to take the next obvious course and attempt to hide away in the Broken Hills. He kept straight on to the eastward, down Running Man, crossing Snowbird Creek near its mouth.

By midnight he was riding in a wild tumble of bleak, snow-burdened hills north of Camas. A hundred men might ride for days unseen in this rough country, and even if the search had already begun, he was fairly safe from pursuit.

But there was no immediate hurry, he knew. Until that warrant was taken to his place, he was not supposed to know that he was in jeopardy. When they found he had gone, they would ride in haste to the border to seek news of him there. And the snow was three days old, gouged and shifted by the wind. By the feel of the air, there was promise of more. Not even bloodhounds could follow his trail after that.

When the wilderness had him deep hidden and the young moon had dropped out of sight behind a pine-covered butte he had passed an hour before, he searched for a sheltered nook in a wooded gulch and camped for the night. He even permitted himself the luxury of a bright fire of pine branches which lighted his immediate surroundings gloriously. By the flickering glow of it he unsaddled Hawk and spared a blanket for his sweaty back. Then, with the tarp to turn the wind and protect him from the frozen ground, he rolled himself in the other blanket, spread his fur coat over all and slept with not even a dream to trouble him.

CHAPTER TWENTY-ONE

"HE'S NOT IN HIS ROOM AT ALL," SUSAN ANNOUNCED pettishly, at nine o'clock next morning. "He didn't sleep there last night, either. He must have gone up to Than's last night for something and didn't come back."

"Well, that's no reason why he should dilly-dally up there all forenoon when he knows the chores ought to be done," Mom scolded, pushing back the coffeepot which she had for two hours been trying to keep hot without letting it boil; an almost impossible feat, since she needed a hot oven. She finished crimping the edges of her mince pies with a steel fork.

"I s'pose I might as well milk and be done with it, so the cow can be turned out into the corral. You watch them pies, Baby, and keep up the fire. But don't put in more'n one stick of wood at a time—and turn 'em around every few minutes, so they'll brown even." Meaning the pies.

Susan watched her mother fold the large brown shawl she always wore in cold weather and pull it down over her wrinkled forehead, tucking it neatly in at the sides and pinning it under her chin with a safety pin. When she had gone scurrying to the stable with the milk bucket, Susan returned to Dade's room and stood looking around the small place with its book-filled shelves, its couch bed in one corner by a window, a homemade reading chair by the other.

It was Dade's retreat, his sanctuary from the irritations of his little world. Beyond a weekly cleaning, Susan did little to keep it in order, yet it was immaculate with a military precision in the orderly arrangements of Dade's belongings. Old-maidish, Susan called it; yet it intrigued her just as his room at home in Great Falls had always done when she was ten and never could pass his door without slipping in to gaze and touch this thing and that. While never putting it in so many words, Dade's room always wore an air of mystery. It seemed aloof from the family, almost secretive.

So now she could look about her and name what objects were missing. His rifle, for instance, and two boxes of shells that always had stood on the shelf just beneath the antlers where he kept the gun. And there were other things, she discovered, when she looked in his wardrobe and chest of drawers. An extra suit of heavy underwear; his high felt pacs and the heavy socks that went inside, and the overshoes he always wore over them. That footgear he never wore except in blizzards or when he must take a long ride in the cold. Certainly not for a mile ride up to Than's shack. And when she felt the bed, the coverings seemed thinner.

While her mother was gone, Susan did more than attend to the mince pies in the oven. She dressed for riding. By the time Mom came in with the foamy bucket of milk, Susan had her white stocking cap pulled well down over her ears and was pulling on her fleece-lined gloves.

"I took out two of the pies; the other one isn't brown enough," she said. "I'm going up to Than's and rout those fellows out. If I'm not back right away, you'll know I've gone down to meet Jean. She said she'd come early and help me decorate the table. Or I may go to meet Blaney, if I see him coming. In other words," she finished, rather breathlessly, "I'm just spoiling for a ride, Mommie."

"Well, run along, Baby. And tell those boys for mercy sake to get themselves down here, where I'll be sure of 'em. I can't have 'em scurruping off somewhere just as I get ready to put the dinner on the table. I can't see what's keeping Blaney, either."

"Oh, he'll come. We sent up to the Falls for a big box of stuff from the Kandy Kitchen; nuts and stuffed dates and all their different kinds of candy. That's partly what he went in for. So if it hadn't come, he was going to wait for the night express. I told them to make it a rush order, so they'd send it, all right. I won't be gone very long, Mom."

Mom was busy at the moment straining the milk, so Susan escaped without being questioned or hindered.

She was back in a surprisingly short time. She came white-faced into the cabin, shut the door and leaned against it, looking at her mother with big frightened eyes.

Mom looked up from stuffing the turkey. "My conscience, Baby! What on earth's the matter with

172

you?"

Susan took a long breath. "Than's gone too," she blurted. "It—I guess they're all right, but Bearnson and another man and Blaney came just as I was looking around to see if Than had taken the same kind of stuff Dade took. They were looking for Than. And Blaney told me I better hurry on home and tell you not to worry and it'll be all right. It's something about the Tepee cattle, I think. Mr. Bearnson looked awful mad because Than wasn't there."

"Don't you go and mister old Pete to me," Mom admonished, and went on crowding sage-and-onion dressing into the turkey. When it would hold no more, she sewed up the cavity with crinkled white twine plainly filched from an empty floursack, bound the drumsticks deftly together and pinioned the wings down close to the sides. Beneath one wing she tucked the liver; under the other went the gizzard, while Susan watched in complete silence.

Mom turned and a white line showed around her mouth; the little betraying sign of repressed emotion which Than had inherited from her. "I ain't a mite su'prised," she said. "I've been expectin' old Pete to make some such move, after Thannie burned them haystacks. Most likely the boys got wind of something and 've pulled out to save a killin'. I don't know where they git their yellow streak from. It ain't from their father or me, I know that. The Robertses never run from trouble before. But it's likely they've got something in their mind 't they're goin' t' do. We won't misjudge 'em; they're pritty sharp, both of 'em. Old Pete Bearnson'll have to git up early to git ahead of either one of 'em."

The crunching of feet in the path halted her boastings.

173

"You open the door, Baby. I've got to wash my hands. Let 'em in—we'll see what they've got to say for themselves."

It was Blaney who entered first. The other two waited outside. Blaney put an arm around Susan, drew her close to his side. But his eyes were turned upon Mom.

"Where's Dade? And Than? Do you know, Mom?"

"If I did, I wouldn't tell that skunk outside there. Who's that with him? What do they think they want of my boys?" Mom's challenging voice was clearly audible to the two waiting just beyond the doorstep.

"It's the sheriff, Mom. There seems to be a pretty bad mix-up over some stock. The Tepee found some of their cattle—a few of that Pothook brand they own—with the brands altered to Cross N's. They're after Than for it, but they think Dade must know something about it too. They've got warrants for both. Than seems to have skipped, from the look of things."

"I don't know where David is. You can let the sheriff come in and look for himself, but I ain't going to have old Pete prowlin' around my premises, and you can tell 'im I said so. You tell 'im if he sets a foot inside that door, I'll scald 'im."

"I don't think he wants to, Mom." Blaney opened the door, beckoned the sheriff inside. "Mrs. Roberts, this is Sheriff Mullen. Mrs. Roberts suggested that you look through the house, Sheriff."

"Matter of form, Mrs. Roberts." The sheriff was a tall bulky man with a red face and chin whiskers that just escaped being red. When he removed his fur cap he revealed sandy hair sleekly plastered to his head with moisture from the close warm cap. His manner was mild, deprecating in the extreme.

"In there's David's room," Mom said tartly. "He ain't

174

in it but you can take a look and see for yourself. I sent my daughter in to call him and he wasn't there. That's all I know about it."

"My duty to look around," the sheriff muttered embarrassedly and stepped within Dade's room.

Blaney stepped over to Mom by the wash bench, taking Susan with him. He thrust a folded paper into Mom's hands which she was drying on the kitchen towel.

"I found it in Than's shack, sticking in the spout of the teakettle. The others didn't see it, so you needn't say anything about it if you think it's best not to."

"What—"

"Dade left it for Than; last night probably. I don't know when Than left, but he was gone when Dade got there and he hasn't been back." He looked at her, suddenly slipped an arm around her shoulders. "I needn't tell you they're like my own brothers. I'll do anything on earth to help. Hurry and read that and tell me what you think of it."

"I sh'll have to git my glasses," she said helplessly. "Here, Baby, you read it quick, before that sheriff comes pokin' his nose in here again."

But Susan was crying. Blaney drooped his head on a level with the two women and read hurriedly in a low tone:

"Put them on my trail and stay with Mom. They can't convict you unless you weaken. Tell them I did it. Don't worry—they'll never catch me."

"It sounds to me like David thinks Jonathan stole them cattle," Mom made bewildered comment. "Baby, stop your bawling! David thinkin' so can't make it so and forty sheriffs snoopin' around don't make my boys thieves." Her fighting spirit began to take control. "I sh'd just like to see them cattle myself," she declared grimly, tucking the note into her apron pocket as the sheriff walked through the room to look into the two Blaney had added to the cabin. "I don't believe a word about them brands bein' worked over into our brand. That's just some lie of old Pete Bearnson's to git my boys in trouble."

"I saw them, Mom," Blaney told her gravely. "I saw Bearnson in Camas last evening, with the sheriff. I rode out with them this morning. They're holding the cattle in a corral at the Tepee. The brands have been worked, no doubt about that. But Than never did it; I'd stake my life on that."

"And what about my David?" Mom demanded sternly. "D' you think for a minute *he* did it?"

The sheriff, entering at that moment, saved Blaney from the embarrassment of replying.

"Uh—Mrs. Roberts, I hope you won't—uh—let this spoil your Thanksgiving," the sheriff said awkwardly. "If I was you, I'd advise the boys to let me serve these warrants. Matter of form, mostly. I—uh—I'll have to take them to town, of course, but no doubt you can furnish bail till the whole thing can be thrashed out in court. Uh—you want to remember that arrest don't mean conviction. Probably they'll be able to clear this matter up without much trouble."

"A course they can," snapped Mom. "My boys ain't thieves, Mr. Sheriff, and all the warrants you can haul out here with a four-horse team of mules don't make a mite of difference. They're innocent. Both of 'em."

"Yes—uh—I don't doubt it in the least. But the law requires that I take them back with me. Uh—can you

176

tell me where I'll be likely to find 'em?"

"No," said Mom shortly, "I can't. They're good boys and they know what they're doing. If they seen fit to pull out, I hope they're both in Canady by this time."

With a sudden access of indignation, she threw open the door and confronted Bearnson, who was waiting on his horse and holding the reins of the sheriff's hired nag.

"And as for *you*, I want you to know I'll clear my boys of this charge if it takes ten years. And when I do, I'll land *you* behind the bars where you belong. If them brands are altered, you know more about it than my boys do. And there is such a thing as a law against conspiracy. Put that in your pipe and smoke it!" She let the sheriff out and slammed the door after him.

"Baby, stop your crying now and put some wood in the stove. I've got to get my turkey in the oven. It's likely the boys 'll be here for dinner. They'll come when they see the coast is clear."

Blaney had followed the sheriff outside. Now he came in looking blank.

"This is the limit!" he exclaimed, looking from one to the other. "The sheriff's a foxy old coot. He just now deputized me to find the boys and bring them in. And I've a sneaking idea they'll have some of the boys from the Tepee on the job too."

"And small good will it do them!" cried Jean, walking in upon them, with her father close behind her. "Oh, I ken fine what it's all about," she added, glancing proudly from one to the other. "Than told me yesterday, and I brought Father early, so that he could talk it over with ye before the sheriff came. But I see them riding away empty-handed. Did they no' take Dade, then?"

Blaney leaned, gently pulled the paper from Mom's pocket and gave it to Jean. "Dade's gone and so is

Than," he said quietly. "I found this up in Than's cabin a little while ago."

Jean paled, but she read the note, frowned and read it a second time. "Here, Father, read it."

She gave Susan's hand a squeeze, went over and put her arms around Mom's neck. "The turkey'll maybe stick in our throats—an' the twa lads away," she said, with a gallant smile. "But it could be far worse. It could be that they're guilty. For now mark ye, Than went away to save Dade from suffering the penalty. He thinks Dade is the one did it; he told me so. And Dade went away thinking Than the guilty one! If thae note was found in Than's cabin, then Than was gone before Dade came to him. Oh, it's a fine muddle they've made of it!

"But they didna change those brands, that much is plain; for I talked with Than and Dade has told what he thinks in the note. And now, Father and Blaney, here's work for the two o' ye! Work for us all. We've to find *who* altered those brands. Ay, stare at the wall all ye like, Father—your brain works slow, but it's the keenest in the country for a' that—present company no' excepted."

Blaney and MacHardie exchanged glances behind Jean's back. MacHardie, a silent man by nature, methodically began removing his fur coat and overshoes, then found his pipe and began filling it from a leather pouch intricately twisted to hold it shut when not in use.

Blaney hunched his shoulders. "It must be great to be a woman," he observed ambiguously.

"And why, then?" Jean demanded suspiciously.

"Oh, because a woman can settle all the problems of the universe by intuition," Blaney retorted glumly. "They never have to bother with reason and logic and

178

all those masculine limitations."

"Mon, ye're richt aboot that," MacHardie agreed solemnly. They were the first words he had spoken within the room and they were the only words he spoke until he was asked to say grace at the table, three hours later.

CHAPTER TWENTY-TWO

A BITTER THING IT IS TO WAIT, UNABLE TO DO anything to help our own in their trouble. With suspense always at her elbow by day and with fear for her bedfellow at night, Mom Roberts grew hollow-eyed and haggard. There were times when she spoke of herself as a friendless old woman whose life was ending in sorrow and shame. There were more times when she threatened to hitch up and drive over to the Tepee and give old Pete Bearnson a piece of her mind; which fortunately remained from day to day an empty threat.

Could she have fought openly for her boys, she would have gloried in the fray; but this waiting and watching, the uncertainty and the fear, heaped too high a burden upon her back. A stooped peering look of age was coming upon her before its time. Always when the wind blew cold at night, or when whirling snowflakes fell from clouds ominously gray and lowering, a drawn pinched look would come into her face and her eyes would have a hunted stare when she looked out across the bleak valley.

Blaney did what he could. But even Susan was growing red-eyed and listless, full of resentment against powers she could not control. With things like this, she openly shirked her sewing. What was the use? They

179

couldn't have any double wedding on Christmas day; not with one of the prospective bridegrooms hiding out in the hills somewhere and the sheriff hunting him as if he were a train robber or something. And with Dade gone too, the house was about as cheerful as a graveyard. She didn't see how Jean MacHardie could stand having Than living like an animal in the woods somewhere. She knew if it were Blaney, she'd simply go crazy.

Jean puzzled more than Susan. Somehow she clung to her optimism. Because Than would like it if he knew, she "kept the bagpipes squealing" more or less consistently in her talk. She kept the trail well traveled between her home and the Roberts' cabin, and she held long, earnest conversations with Blaney, who had managed to persuade Bearnson and the sheriff that he was of more use to the law, there at the ranch, than he would be out hunting without clues. The Roberts boys, he declared, would be sure to show up sooner or later at home. Jean worried him a little. She had become obsessed by a fixed idea that both Than and Dade were innocent, the victims of a deliberate conspiracy to drive them out of the country or send them to the penitentiary. She believed Bearnson himself was the man who had altered those brands. At least, that is what she believed nearly all of the time. She harried Blaney without mercy, telling him what she would do if she were a man, able to play the detective and gather evidence that would convict the guilty party; or parties.

Blaney believed that Dade was guilty and that dues were best left alone. What would she do if he gathered evidence that would convict Dade?

Jean maintained that Dade's note proved beyond a doubt that he thought Than was guilty; and would

180

Blaney tell her how he could think that if he himself were the one? Or perhaps he thought the two of them were in it together!

No, Blaney did not think that. The whole Tepee outfit might swear they saw Thane do it—caught him in the act of altering the brands. Blaney still wouldn't believe it. Their testimony would merely prove they were a bunch of damned liars.

"But still you must admit the cows never branded themselves by any chance?" she argued one day, when she arrived to find him busy currying his saddle horse. "Some hand held the iron to their sides for them. Ye'll no' deny that, wull ye?"

Blaney laughed, meeting the dazzle of her big pupiled blue eyes with due appreciation of their beauty. "No, I'll no' deny that," he mimicked. "You said yesterday you had decided Bearnson must have passed the job on to some one else. Who are you seeing in the part now? Me? Or is it your father?"

"There are juist twa men I do *not* see in the part," she retorted, "an' they're both in hiding." She looked at him in sober wistfulness. "I have a theory, Blaney, and if ye were fair and impartial an' willing to go to any length to learn the truth, I might tell it ye."

"Let's have it, Jean. Anything that can possibly help–—"

"If ye felt as I do, there'd be not even that condition put upon your assistance. How can ye know it willna help, until it's been tried? With my Thannie sleeping out in the storms, and maybe hungry and sick, and with no place he dare go for comfort, one wad think ye'd try everything ye can think of; even to getting yon Bearnson by the throat and choking the truth from him." She set her teeth hard together, turning away her face

181

lest he see how her eyes were brimming.

Blaney flushed. He knocked the currycomb against the stable door to free it of hair. "You know there's nothing I wouldn't do to clear this thing up," he said. "Aside from the boys, this is raising Cain with the rest of us. There's no sacrifice too great for me to make—if only I knew *what* to do. I don't get after Bearnson, simply because I don't believe he knows any more about it than we do. He's a darn good actor if he does. I think it was Dade, wanting to get even with the Tepee. I can follow his line of reasoning, all right. He was simply collecting damages without going through the formality of suing."

"Oh, ay, I can see the argument. But he didna do it."

Blaney gave an impatient sigh. "You say yourself that they didn't brand themselves, and it doesn't look reasonable to me that some one else did it. Bearnson you can count out, so far as I'm concerned. His mind is all taken up with making money in the cattle business. His thoughts run in accepted channels. He'd no more put the Roberts brand on his own stock than he'd hamstring them and leave them for the wolves. Fight, yes. But not where he's risking half a dozen cows with their calves."

"Ye may think it—"

"I certainly do. If he set a trap for the boys, to get them in trouble, he wouldn't use his own stock for bait; I know him well enough for that."

"Somebody did it," Jean said stubbornly.

"Yes. And if we didn't know these boys, if Than were a perfect stranger, we'd take it for granted he's the one who did. We'd say he took the chance of some one seeing those brands before they haired over, and that he lost. We're prejudiced in his favor—I realize all that.

And yet I'd stake my life on his innocence."

"And what about Dade, then?"

"Oh, Dade—" Blaney's shoulders twitched in spite of himself. "Well, it takes experience to rope and tie down a cow. He never handled a rope in his life until they took up these claims and bought a few head of stock. But he's been doing a lot of riding around lately. Still, if you insist that he couldn't do the work alone, that brings us right around to Than again."

"It does not!"

"It does if we're logical," Blaney persisted. "It's because we won't be logical that we keep talking in circles. We know in our own hearts Than had nothing to do with it. But you must admit that the evidence all says that he did have everything to do with it. I can't accept the evidence, that's all. Neither will you."

"I'll no' bandy wurrds wi' ye," Jean said crossly and turned as if she would leave him.

"Oh, but you didn't tell me this new theory yet," Blaney reminded her, thrusting the currycomb into a convenient crack in the wall and sending his glossy-coated horse out into the corral where he immediately rolled and spoiled his looks. "Let's have the idea. It may be just the thread that will unravel the whole case. Don't be spiteful, Jean."

Her face showed signs of relenting and she did not go on to the house, but still she did not answer him, but stood staring abstractedly down the creek. There a new, light snowfall hid all the ugly black patches of meadow and field and the willows were frosted fairy woods. By the look in her eyes, she did not see them at all.

"No word from Than, is there?"

Jean shook her head. "I'm no' expecting any. He's in the hills, I haven't a doubt."

183

"The sheriff thinks they went together and that they headed north," Blaney observed, though the subject had been gone over many times. "What's the new theory?"

"Well, I'll not tell it ye. I'll work it out by myself somehow. You'd but muddle it with your skepticism and we'd get nowhere at all."

"Well, that would be as far as we've got these two weeks—and are likely to get, as far as I can see," Blaney said bluntly.

"Certainly ye'll get nowhere, as long as ye bide here feeding the cow and brushing down your saddle horse and carrying in wood so ye can sit by the fire o' nights," Jean cried bitterly. "If ye would clear this black mystery and let Than come back to his home again—get ye gone from here, Blaney King! Father can spare a man to do these few chores for the women."

Blaney gave her a quick, almost a startled look that held in it a question.

This she answered fiercely. "Ye're like a man with his blankets pulled over his head. Get out where ye can see and hear what's going on, why don't ye?"

"Oh, good Lord!" gasped Blaney. "Where—"

"Get ye over to the Tepee! Say that ye've quarreled with Susan and her mither, you thinkin' the boys are guilty and the women turnin' ye out for your opeenion. Say—say *anything,* mon, only so ye convince them the Robertses are no more your friends."

Blaney stared at her. "And is *that* your theory?"

Jean but tossed her head at him and started up the hard-packed path to the house. Before she had passed out of easy speaking distance however, she turned and looked back at him.

"Man, man, have ye lived in the West so long, and yet do not see how much a man can learn by sitting with

184

open ears over a card game, perhaps, in a bunk house?"

She went on to the cabin then and went in without once looking back. When she had disappeared from view, Blaney went back to his chores which Jean so despised.

"That girl would accuse her grandfather's ghost if she thought it would bring Than home," he muttered angrily. But presently he was thinking of what she had said. The things one might learn in a bunk house. The girl was nobody's fool, after all. It might, he told himself grudgingly, be worth while to try it and see what he could dig up.

CHAPTER TWENTY-THREE

BY THE HUSHED, BREATHLESS SILENCE OF THE HILLS, BY the carven stillness of the bull pines in the jagged ravines which led steeply up from the narrow coulee bottom wherein he rode, by the slaty sky and the heavy air that held a deceptive warmth, Than knew of the coming blizzard some hours before it arrived.

For more than two weeks he had been wandering more or less at random through the hills to the north of the Missouri. He had passed Chinook, giving it a wide berth and swinging south just where he might be expected to go north or east. The Little Rockies would shelter him almost indefinitely, he knew. He was not the first man to live a retired life among them—and for that very reason, because it was notorious as a hang-out for fugitive lawbreakers, he was beginning to find it irksome.

Furthermore, if he were followed with the zeal one would expect Bearnson to demand of the law, here was one place where they would look for him; warily, on the chance that he held life more cheaply than his own liberty. Most men did, when affairs took a turn that sent them riding in haste to the Little Rockies. The narrow twisting canyons and rocky pinnacles seemed diabolically contrived for easy ambush, and a man with a rifle and plenty of ammunition need never be taken so long as he was careful.

But the Law might take advantage of those secret nooks too. It was a game that could be played two ways. So Than rode on guard, as it were. When Hawk's ears tilted forward inquiringly Than's eyes followed the signal which was plain as a pointed finger. He met full and close the startled gaze of a black-tailed buck, and with his six-shooter brought it tumbling down the slope.

Here was meat to last him through the blizzard. With a sheltered nook and firewood in plenty, he would be able to weather the storm in primitive comfort; for after all, the necessities of life may be trimmed down in a pinch to food, drink and warmth. Than's hard-muscled health bore witness to the truth of this. He was leaner, but he was tough as a wolf.

He dismounted, dragged the deer down the remaining ten feet of slope and called Hawk to him, meaning to lift his kill across the saddle and go on to find a snug camping place. With the hunter's instinct, he lifted the antlered head and looked to see where his bullet had struck.

Just under the muzzle it had entered, angling up through the brain and out at the back of the head three inches or so behind the ears. A pretty shot, clean and true, leaving the body unmarred. He glanced back at the sleek sides and rump which promised a full stomach for himself for days to come

With a grunt of dismay, he dropped the head and stared hard at what he saw. The barrel of the buck should have been sleek and full. It was not. In the flank, just missing the rump, was a bleeding wound as fresh almost as his own shot, judging by the unclotted blood flowing from the bullet hole.

Than knelt and examined the wound incredulously. By no freak of ricochet could his bullet have entered that flank. Coming out behind the ears at an upward slant, it had gone on up the hillside somewhere and landed in the thick brush. Another bullet, from another gun, had made that wound in the flank.

A man does not wander for two weeks alone in the wilderness without feeling a keen sense of isolation. Than's blood felt like ice in his veins. Could it be that he was being followed, dogged day after day, while he loitered through these hills, leisurely debating with himself whether he should go or stay? He stood up, his rifle in his hands, suddenly suspicious of every rock and tree, every jutting ledge within sight.

Warned again by Hawk's upflung head and his eyes staring up the slope, Than stepped back and peered up the hillside, his rifle at half aim. What he saw was the thin, querulous face of Dade, staring down at him in astonished disapproval.

"Might I ask what the devil *you're* doing away down here?" Dade parted the bushes and came down, digging his heels in the yellow gravel to save himself the discomfort of descending with a rush.

"Well, good glory! Where did *you* drop down?" Than gasped.

Dade lifted ironical eyebrows at the dead buck. "I suppose you finished him," he remarked. "I only got a running shot a mile or so back." He looked at Than

187

curiously. "Well, how many did you bring along with you?"

"Hunh? How many what?" Than blurted, staring angrily.

"Why, men. You must be making a very thorough job of it, dear brother, taking the trail yourself. Now you can claim the credit for haling me—"

"Hale hell!" Than snorted. "Why ain't you home where you belong? What you doing, prowling around down here?"

"Now, don't get excited," Dade expostulated. "Where's your posse? I hope you've brought a cook along. After a straight meat diet, I'd certainly appreciate one good meal."

Than's expression changed from bewilderment to gloom. "When did *you* pull out?" he demanded bluntly.

"Is it possible you don't know? That note I left should have told you. As a matter of fact, I left the night before Thanksgiving. About midnight, I should judge. You were off courting, apparently." He gave his twisted smile. "Fiddling while Rome burned, so to speak."

Than ignored the thrust. He never did have much patience with Dade in his more supercilious moods. He was angry, alarmed, disappointed. It seemed to him now that his two weeks of hiding had been utterly useless.

"Hell, I took it for granted you'd have sense enough to stay, if I pulled out," he said bluntly. "Why in thunder didn't you stand pat? They couldn't prove a thing against you if you hadn't lost your nerve and beat it.

"What did you want to be such a sneaking coward for? Haven't I always taken the hard knocks for you? Couldn't you see that with me gone, they wouldn't have enough evidence against you to tangle the hind leg of a fly? They'd think I did it. Now," he almost shouted, "they think we were *both* in on it!"

"You seem to forget, dear brother—"

"I don't forget anything, you lean-livered little runt! I could kick you from here to the ranch and I would too, if I thought it would do any good. You go and sneak off like this—and you didn't have to! D' you get that? Nobody suspected you. They all thought—why, even Dilly, and he's as good a friend as I've got—even Dilly thought I did it!"

Dade stood facing him calmly, his exasperating little smile on his lips. But they were bloodless, as was his thin, querulous face.

"Well—and didn't you do it?"

Than's mouth dropped open, though he made no sound at all. He just stared.

"You see," Dade continued, in that cold, biting way he had at times, "your reasoning is all very logical, but it happened that I reasoned from another premise. Like Dilly, I felt very sure that you had done it. Just as I was sure you had burned some of Bearnson's hay."

"Burned—you mean to say *you* didn't burn them stacks?"

"Those, dear brother? No, I thought you were having revenge in rather an ignoble way. Just as the altering of those brands was a low form of revenge. And in a mistaken mood of brotherly responsibility, I reasoned that you are strong and likely to live to a good old age. Also, you were about to marry a nice girl—though too buoyant for my taste—on Christmas; I did not believe you to be essentially a criminal mind—"

"Say, good glory! I'll—"

"One moment. While we are on the subject, let me finish. I reasoned that I am not looking forward to marriage—thank God. My health is nothing to boast about. It occurred to me that if I should suddenly disappear, it would naturally start the hue and cry in my direction. I think I rather wanted the experience of sacrificing myself on the family altar. I never had, you know. It would be a novelty. Furthermore, no man who knew me at all would believe that anything less than a guilty fear of being caught and convicted for my crime would drive me off in the dead of winter—without my cough syrup too!"

Than swallowed dryly. "Boiled down, I suppose that means you didn't work those brands?"

Dade gave a gentlemanly sniff. "Not unless I have formed a disagreeable habit of branding cattle in my sleep!" He laughed mirthlessly. "Did you?"

"Hell, no! I thought it was you."

A peculiar look, almost a twinkle, was in Dade's eyes. "Remembering certain comments you made on my ignorance of ropes, cows and branding irons last fall," he drawled, "I suppose I may consider that suspicion as a backhanded compliment. Do you recall telling me that I handled a branding iron like an old woman crocheting lace?"

Than grinned briefly. "You do too," he maintained. "I did kinda wonder how you managed to get 'em on right side up."

A few snowflakes wafted down between the two. Than looked up at the ominous gray clouds, shook his head and stooped to the buck, hunting knife open in his hand. "Can't stand here chewing the rag about it now," he observed. "Have to hunt shelter pretty darned *pronto*. It's going to storm."

"I've taken possession of an old cabin I found in a little basin just around this ridge," Dade offered. "Unless you've got something better, suppose we hustle

190

over there. The devil himself couldn't find it in a storm."

"You're a chump to take possession of anything down here when you're on the dodge," Than commented, with brotherly freedom. "What if the owner walked in on you?"

"I scarcely think he will," Dade replied. "In fact, I'm practically sure he won't. I carried his bones out and buried them before I moved in."

Than gave a surprised grunt but he had nothing to say. With the antlered head removed, they threw the buck across the saddle and tied it there. Dade led the way into a narrow, rocky defile which ascended rather steeply to a shoulder of the ridge; then down the other side to a scrubby thicket where he had left his horse while he followed the buck. From there he took the lead up a tributary canyon that grew deeper, narrower and more choked with timber, until at last it widened into a tiny basin, flat-bottomed, brushy in spots, secluded as the most retiring of mortals could desire.

"It's in here somewhere," Dade announced, with a tinge of pride in his tone. "I've lived here for a week, but whenever I leave the place, getting back is a guessing contest."

"Well, it's a dandy hide-out," Than agreed when, after a half hour's wandering, he found the cabin by bumping into the rock chimney. "What about the horses? Do we have to take them inside with us?"

Dade laughed slightly, as if in a detached, impersonal way he rather enjoyed the unusual situation. "There's a sheltered rock corral made to order, back against the hill. Grass in it and a warm spring. Grass is green, mind you. I'll take the horses up there. I think you had better stay here and give a yell now and then, so I can find the way back. Tomorrow I'll show you the natural advantages of the place."

But on the morrow Than opened the crude door upon a dense shifting wall of powdery snow, with occasional dark blurs which he knew to be trees and bushes growing almost within reach of his hand. He slammed the door against the icy cold of the blizzard and turned back gratefully to the fire.

With his naturally careful attention to detail, Dade had gathered a great stack of dry wood. One end of the cabin—the end where he had found the dry bones of his predecessor, as he whimsically explained—was filled to the roof with sound pine branches, pitch knots from logs of fallen trees. There had been an axe, gun, a few cooking utensils, he told Than. He had no compunctions whatever about using them; except the gun, which was fowled and rusty.

Three days the blizzard raged. They did not talk much of the stolen cattle after that first evening's discussion. Dade spent hours on end reading by the light of the fire. On the evening of the second day he read aloud to Than. Shakespeare, of all books! Than had often seen that worn little book with its ruinously fine print. Dade carried it in his pocket quite often. Now he read all of Hamlet, during which Than visioned Dade himself as the gloomy Dane. He seemed to live the part as he read, keeping the other characters back in the shadows, mere wraithlike creatures serving the character he so evidently loved.

This was a new Dade; one whom Than had never discovered until now. All his life afterward, whenever he thought of that storm and the hidden cabin down in the Little Rockies, he always saw Dade pacing the dismal halls of a castle, cynically planning vengeance

192

for his father's troubled ghost. He rather admired the character, or rather, Dade in the character. It gave him an odd glamor in Than's eyes. It almost overshadowed the fine sacrifice Dade had attempted to make for him.

On the fourth morning they awoke to a world dazzling white, still as the calm which lies brooding upon the shrouded figure of one dead. They broiled venison steak, brewed strong tea and drank it to the grounds. Then Than rose and stretched his arms to the low rafters, brought them down and looked at Dade.

"I'm going back home and see what's doing," he announced. "I'll leave you most of the plunder. You'd no business to pull out the way you did, without leave or license. You might have come to me first."

"I did go to you. I went up right after Frank Hoskins told me. One of the Tepee boys had told him, and he rode over immediately. He told me I'd better warn you. He thought, of course, you were guilty, just as I did when I heard about it. But on account of Jean, he was afraid you would not take too kindly to anything he might say if he went to you direct. So he came to me and I hurried right up to your place. But you were off down the creek as usual."

"I thought you said it was about midnight when you rode up to my place."

Dade smiled his twisted smile. "That, dear brother, was the second time I visited you. When I went home after my first attempt, I was pretty much disgusted with you—going blandly about your love-making with that cattle-stealing hanging over your head, so to speak. It was later in the evening that I decided to sacrifice my humble self upon the family altar and shame you into living a purer, nobler life."

"Oh, cut it out. You can't rub that in. Just remember

193

I'm down here because I thought *you* done it."

"Did, Jonathan. You're getting terribly slipshod in your grammar. And I think, since I am considered merely an ignorant accomplice at best—or worst—you'd better let me go."

"Not on your life! I'm not going to raise the long howl to let all the neighbors know I'm back. I'm going to do an Injun crawl, so to speak. I want to see Blaney and tell him how the thing stacks up and let Mom and Jean know we're all right. I'll be back in a week or so. Anything you want me to bring yuh?"

"Well," said Dade, "you might bring me Spencer's First Principles, and a pie. And if you're not too loaded, you could slip my copy of Henley, or maybe Shelley, into your pocket. They're both little fellows, no trouble at all—but mighty good company when a feller's all alone."

Than looked down at him with a new understanding and sympathy. "Don't you worry, old boy. I'll bring 'em all. You better stay inside. Be good to yourself—you and Shakespeare hold 'er down till I get here."

They clasped hands briefly, almost furtively. Then Than picked up his bridle, shouldered his saddle and blanket and left the cabin.

CHAPTER TWENTY-FOUR

SEEMINGLY TRIVIAL INCIDENTS WERE WEAVING A pattern of vital significance elsewhere that day, when the great storm lay brooding over the northern ranges waiting for the moment to strike. In Camas, Dilly and Frank Hoskins were walking with the sprung-kneed gait of dyed-in-the-wool cowpunchers down the street, when they met Blaney coming out of the Klondyke saloon just as they were turning to go in.

Dilly grabbed him by the arm, would have swung him around facing the other way, except that Blaney stood firm where he was.

"Aw, come on back," Dilly urged. "You can't break back on us this way, Blaney."

"Nothing doing in there, boys. One old sheep herder in there playing solitaire and two farmers are talking politics. The barkeep's having a nap and doesn't want to be disturbed. That's why I came out."

"Why, the dirty, low-lived skunk!" Dilly denounced. "Havin' a nap, is he? Well now, I'll nap 'im!"

"Oh, come on, Dilly." Blaney's grip tightened. "Let's hit the trail for home."

"No, sir, I'm goin' in and wake up that son-of-a-gun of a barkeep that thinks he's got nothin' to do but sleep. I'll show him where to head in at, the lousy loafer. I'll have him jumpin' four ways at once—"

"Look! I've got all you need right here." Blaney showed the sag of his overcoat pocket. "If that isn't enough, I know where there's another. We've got to drift, boys. It's going to storm."

"Aw, I won't be more'n a minute," Dilly argued. "Come on. Le's have just one apiece—one, mind yuh— and then I'll go. Honest."

"Nothing doing, Dilly. I've got all we need to see us home happy as a lark. Don't you believe it?" He tilted his overcoat pocket until the neck of a ribbed bottle showed plainly.

Frank Hoskins smiled and tilted his own pocket. "I've got the mate to it," he boasted, "and another inside my shirt, in case this gets busted or leaks or something. Come on, Dilly. We'll all go broke if we lay over two three days."

"Oh, all right," Dilly yielded reluctantly. "What's that in your other pocket, Blaney? Another bottle?"

Blaney laughed in some embarrassment. Being an engaged young man was still something of a novelty. "Candy," he stated truthfully, as the speediest way to finish the discussion. "For the one I love. Two pounds of chocolates in a gold box tied with silver ribbon. Come on, you chump."

"Gee, I wish I'd thought of that," Dilly cried enviously. "Say, wait till I go buy me a box for Mom Roberts. She's sore as hell, but I think a lot of that old gal, no foolin'. Bet nobody ever thinks to buy her candy. Come on back to the store. It won't take but a minute and then I'll start right out. Honest."

That seemed reasonable enough. Blaney nodded and they turned back and walked arm in arm to the store, partly because both were in a mellow mood—Dilly much mellower than Blaney or Frank Hoskins—but chiefly because Blaney wanted no turning aside into other places of refreshment. While Dilly, innocently and because he liked them himself, chose a beflowered box of chewy chocolates for Mom, Frank Hoskins nudged Blaney and tipped a thumb over his shoulder.

Blaney looked that way and got a shock. A man had come in with two or three cardboard placards in his hand. While the two watched, he tacked one to the wall beside the door, and over his left arm Blaney saw that it was a $500 Reward offer for the arrest and conviction of Than Roberts, cattle thief, and David Roberts as accomplice.

He turned his head away, feeling a little sick, and as he did so, his glance fell upon Frank's face. He got another shock, though the cause of it was harder to

196

determine. He might have been mistaken, he thought at once; for he had imagined he saw a look of satisfaction on Frank's face; a look of gloating.

Frank's eyes met his and he shook his head. "Too damn bad. They'll both be hard to catch," he said. "I always liked Dade."

Dilly, raking his pockets for loose change, paid no attention. He was counting nickels, dimes and quarters, trying to make up a dollar and a half, the price of the candy. Blaney lent him four bits which completed the sum and hustled him out. The store suffocated him with that placard on the wall and he did not want Dilly to see it, did not want the useless discussion it would excite in his slightly befuddled condition.

Fifteen miles out from town, a few warning flakes sifted down, blown by an icy breath from out the northwest. Blaney gazed around him, untied his neckerchief and bound it over his ears, pulling up the collar of his fur coat that had seemed burdensome no longer than an hour ago.

"She's comin', all right," Dilly cried, in an astonished tone. "My gosh, I thought you was draggin' me outa town so as to save money! We better hit the high spots, I'm tellin' yuh right now!"

"We'll never make it home before dark," Blaney warned. "If I know the signs, this won't be any tame snowstorm. It's a real old blizzard we're up against, boys; the kind you read about in the papers. One of those murdering storms that freeze sheep in bunches and pile cattle up against cutbanks and fences."

"And that's no dream," Dilly declared, now quite sober. "Guess I'll tie up my ears too. Yuh notice how cold it's getting a'ready?"

"What we better do," Frank Hoskins suggested, "is
197

ride up this draw on ahead here, and hit that line camp over the next ridge. You know the one, Dilly. There used to be a stove and a few things in it. And it stands in an alder thicket. I tell yuh right now, boys, I don't want to chance it up around Buffalo Butte."

"Line camp it is," Blaney agreed. "No use punishing our horses, even if we don't value our own hides. It'll probably let up by morning; enough so we can make the ranch, anyway."

"It's dark coming on that I don't like," Dilly complained. "Good thing you got them bottles."

"Lead the way, Frank," Blaney told him, as they loped ahead into the wind and whirling flakes that came faster, thicker, as they rode.

"I'll pilot yuh," Dilly said bluntly. "I wintered in that cabin. I oughta know the way to it." He glanced back at them, shielding his face with his hand. "Well, well, prod up them cayuses of yours a little, can't yuh?" he urged impatiently. "We're goin' to have our work cut out for us locating the blamed camp if we don't get a move on."

Blaney and Frank spurred after him up the fast whitening trail, which Dilly's long-legged gray was taking at a swift gallop. Dusk was creeping upon them, a dusk of swirling snow and of cutting wind that stung their faces and chilled their very blood with its icy cold.

"Good thing we haven't far to go," Blaney ejaculated once, when his horse slipped in a bad part of the trail and recovered himself just in time to save Blaney a nasty fall.

"We're lucky if we get there," Dilly shouted back, and reined short off into a wide draw that led into the farther hills almost at right angles to the road.

It was at about this time that Than and Dade reached their snug shelter many miles to the southeast of Camas.

198

On the high bare ridge which they must cross, the wind caught them full front; Dilly shivered within his big fur coat and led the way at a pace plainly betraying his uneasiness. "I wish we'd of stayed in town," he grumbled once, when Blaney pounded up beside him. "It'd take all the brush in the coulee to keep that shack warm enough so we won't freeze solid."

Blaney made no reply. He was thinking of that placard on the store wall and of the glimpse he had caught of Frank Hoskins' face. He was wondering too how he could get at the thing behind that fleeting expression. It had never struck him before that Frank harbored any jealousy of Than. He had seemed very philosophical about it. But down underneath his philosophy he must feel differently. Certainly he had looked as though he were glad to see that placard going up in a conspicuous place in Camas.

Oh, well, Blaney supposed that was only a perfectly human reaction. He pushed the matter from him and gave all his attention to keeping Dilly in sight.

They fought their way forward, rod by rod. In the fast falling snow the night crept closer, dimming the white blur of the storm. To a certain degree, their experience paralleled that of the fugitives. They were lucky enough to find the cabin, a gray blotch in the swirl of wind-driven snow. The shed for the horses was intact and stood close by. They led them inside, removed the bridles, loosened the cinches and closed the door. The horses would go hungry that night, but they would not freeze.

A few sticks of wood were in the box behind the rusty stove. Blaney started a fire while Dilly and Frank went out and found wood. A near-by corral of heavy poles they fell upon with the axe left inside the cabin, tearing down two panels of the fence and dragging the poles inside. When the end struck the opposite wall, Dilly would chop the pole in two just within the doorway, heave the pole aside and drag in the other half, while Frank went after more. A crude but speedy method of insuring a necessary fuel supply which could be chopped as needed. Dilly was openly pleased with the idea.

Thus fortified against the cold, they grouped themselves around the stove, pulled the cork from a round-ribbed bottle and drank from it in turn. After awhile Dilly sighed, pulled the box of candy from his pocket and solemnly broke the string. Each dipped fingers into the box, slipped pieces of tough candy between their teeth and chewed quite as solemnly as they had drunk. They had reason enough for their gravity; the situation, while not dangerous, certainly did not seem funny to them. At least, it did not in that first hour.

By Blaney's watch, it was nearing midnight. One of the ribbed bottles was empty, a second was showing clear glass to within an inch or two of the bottom. Dilly had sung all the songs he could remember; one song, which recounted the immoral adventures of Sam Bass, he had sung twice, Frank Hoskins joining him at intervals between drinks. Blaney, who was not drinking a third as much as he pretended, did not sing at all.

Frank reached for more candy, laughed at a sudden thought. "If I had my fiddle, boys, we could dance. Remember that dance we had over at Robertses place? That was the first time I noticed anything between my girl and that so-and-so Than Roberts. I was playing a waltz and—say, I knew right then the dirty sneak was going to try and cut me out!"

Blaney gave him a quick look. "I'm sorry you—" He

200

checked himself. It was hardly consistent with the attitude he was taking toward Than and Dade to express any sympathy for them now. He had made it plain to the Tepee boys that he was badly disappointed in the Roberts family, with the single exception of Susan. He wouldn't spoil that now. Dilly was not exactly drunk.

"You're sorry I what?" Frank reached for the nearly empty bottle. "You needn't be sorry for me, old-timer. It takes a smarter man than Than Roberts to get the best of me. I'll tell you that right now." He swallowed three times, sighed with audible satisfaction, pushed in the cork and set the bottle back with a lingering reluctance.

"I'll bet neither one of you would ever guess in a hundred years—" He chuckled to himself, pulled back the bottle and finished its contents. "Kind of a dirty trick, maybe, but hell! They had it coming."

"Hunh?" Dilly roused himself, looked across at Blaney, then leaned and studied Frank's flushed and grinning face. "Tell us, so we can laugh too. What's the joke, Frank?"

Frank stopped laughing to himself, leered at Dilly. "The joke is that I'll have his girl myself before the year's out. Why dammit, I had her cryin' on my shoulder already; coming to me for comfort." He laughed as at a great joke. "Coming to *me*. You get that?" He shook his head owlishly. "No, I guess you wouldn't see the—the sardonic macha-vel—veel— dammit, you know the bird. I'm another. The modern up-to-date macha-what's-his-name."

"You'd have to get up in the morning to beat his time," Blaney observed, artfully doubting.

"I did," Frank stated vaingloriously. "You think, by gosh, because I go around common as an old shoe, I haven't got any brains. You think I'll stand back with my finger in my mouth and let a damned nester step up and take my girl away from me. Or old Bearnson hand me my time right in the middle of spring round-up—"

"You took it," Dilly spoke up, darting a meaning glance at Blaney. "I was there and seen yuh take it and yuh never done a damn thing about it."

"And I've never seen any great play you made to even up the deal with Than Roberts," Blaney added with wily sarcasm.

"You haven't, eh? Say! He's on the dodge, right now. That Christmas wedding is knocked into a cocked hat, ain't it? If he ever shows up around this country, he'll go to the pen so fast it'll make his head swim. Bearnson's hot as hell—and I know why."

"Any bonehead knows that much," Dilly baited him.

"Well, well, Frank's such a wise lad, I guess I'll have to stand treat." Blaney pulled his bottle from his pocket. "Here, Dilly. You and me first."

"Yeah," Dilly fell into the play. "Frank here's been holdin' out on us. Don't let 'im flop a lip over that bottle till he proves he's smarter'n we are. Ain't that right?" He broke the seal, deftly extracted the cork and drank, smacked his lips and passed the bottle back to Blaney.

Blaney smiled across the red-hot stove at Frank.

"Here, Macchiavelli, take a snort and tell us how you worked it."

"Worked what? I never said I worked anything." Frank glared, took the bottle, drank. With a last flicker of caution, he eyed Blaney suspiciously. But the subtle flattery of the name exalted his ego above the possibility of criticism. He laughed suddenly, tickled at a thought.

"Say, Macchiavelli! That's good! Say, I can think circles around that old stiff. If you knew the inside

202

secret dope on Than Roberts—" He laughed again, shook his head as if in amazement at his own cleverness.

"Well," said Blaney, when he had subsided, "If you've got anything cleverer than that old boy, I sure would like to hear it!"

"You think I ain't, do you? Say, listen!"

Frank Hoskins talked. Leaning forward, with his thin, dark face touched furtively now and then by the flickering light from the broken front of the old stove, he explained to the smallest detail why he considered himself smarter than Macchiavelli.

Leaning close, scarcely daring to move, Blaney listened. Once when the fire burned low, Dilly rose carefully, lifted the lid and thrust in another stick as noiselessly as if a sick woman lay asleep in the room. Once Blaney's shaking fingers dropped his sack of tobacco, and when he stooped to recover it, his movement was as carefully unobtrusive as if he feared to frighten some wild creature venturing near. That is how fearful they were of breaking Frank's flow of confidential talk and closing his lips before he had finished.

It was over. Blaney handed him the bottle again, shook his head and laughed. "Well, that certainly does beat anything I ever heard of!" he cried, gazing admiringly at Frank. "Hell, if that were written down, it would go down to posterity as the slickest story of poetic justice ever heard of."

"Damn right," Dilly agreed, showing his teeth in a grin about as friendly as a wolf's. "That sure oughta be wrote up in a book!"

"Have a drink, Frank! Boy, if I had it, you could swim in champagne. My hat's off to you—" He hesitated, gazing at Frank with a puzzled look. "But I don't see how—there's a point or two I don't just *sabe*; just how you worked it out so there was no chance of a slip-up."

Frank waved a condescending hand. "Why, it was like this: I—"

"Just a minute. Damn it, I'm the kinda mark that must have everything down before him in black and white. Hand me that paper you took off the candy box, Dilly. No, I don't want the string, you chump; just the paper. I've got to get this straight. Thanks." He pulled up an extra box, spread the paper upon it, got out his fountain pen which, being new and prized, he had filled in town.

"Now, let's see. First, you got sore at Bearnson because he fired you for kicking your horse in the belly—"

"No. You got that wrong." Frank gazed fatuously over the top of the bottle. "Firsh, I was sore at Than Rob-*hic*-Roberts for tryin' to come between me an' my g-girl. It was bein' shore at Than Ro-Roberts that made me fight my horsh. Tha's why I kicked him in the belly a few times an' got fired. An' thash why I got shore at ole Bearnson. Not s' much for firin' me," he explained carefully, "but for the way he did it. Looked at me like I was a dog. Called me—shay! You know what Bearnson called me? I'll tell you what he called me!"

He did, with blasphemously obscene accuracy. With his face a mask and his fingers steady as steel, Blaney wrote it down.

"Fine. And after he called you that, you decided—"

"I took the matter under ad-vishment," Frank solemnly declared. "I used my head."

While he repeated his boastings, going more into detail than he had done with the first telling (though his articulation was much less clear), Blaney wrote rapidly,

204

skimming the cream of the recital. When he had finished, both sides of the white wrapping paper were nearly covered.

"You'd better sign your name to this, Frank," he purred. "Some damn liar is liable to claim the credit, if you don't."

Drunk though he was on Metropole whisky and his own cleverness, Frank almost balked at that. It took the combined efforts of Blaney and the hard-eyed Dilly to get his Spencerian signature beneath the story. But they got it finally and signed their names as witnesses.

Blaney smoked in absolute silence after that, until Frank had talked himself to sleep, lying curled like a bear in his fur overcoat with his cheek pillowed on the axe handle.

"Now, if he doesn't try to crawfish when we get him to the District Attorney, we're all set," Blaney said finally, dropping his cigarette stub into the stove hearth.

Dilly replied with a sentence not to be repeated. "Let him try it!" he added, through his teeth. "You take that paper straight to the Old Man, Blaney. What he won't do to him!"

"See if he packs a gun, Dilly. He's going back to town with me, soon as this storm lets up, and he's going tied. Mullen didn't make me a deputy sheriff for nothing."

He folded the paper into a neat oblong, unbuckled one high overshoe, pulled off his boot, warmed his foot at the open oven, dropped the paper into his boot and stamped his foot into it. He replaced the overshoe, buckled it and looked at Dilly.

"If the blink-blank-blankety-blank crawls outa that," he gritted, "he'll have to be about a thousand times smarter than he thinks he is!"

CHAPTER TWENTY-FIVE

JEAN BACKED TO THE WALL, TILTED HER HEAD sidewise like an inquisitive robin, nodded and smiled.

"Wi' the beaver coat and the cap pulled down, and wi' that oldish look ye hae till the shoolders, ye're feyther tae the life, lad! With his horse, and if you just go scowling along and say nothing, your own mother wouldn't know ye ten feet away."

She went up and slid both arms around Than in her father's big coat, and hugged him close. "Oh, if ye knew how glad I am to have ye, laddie! Three days and nights while the blizzard was at its worst I was near crazy wi' wondering how ye fared. And now—"

"And I slept in a fairly comfortable cabin with a big fireplace and plenty of dry wood, and ate broiled venison. And listened to Shakespeare's plays. Dade would sure make a fine Hamlet, don't yuh know it?"

"Mon, but ye're that intellectual! And wi' me worriting—"

The door was thrust open, letting in a cloud of congealed air. Jean's father, with no make-believe burr in his voice, called out tartly.

"Mon, mon, dinna ye ken I'm freezin' my taes holdin' yon nags for ye? Come awa'. Dae yer kessin' some ither day, if kess ye wall!"

"Nobody told you to hold the horses," Jean cried, red-cheeked. "Why couldn't you have tied them to the hitch rail, then?"

MacHardie grinned, winked openly at Than and closed the door. Jean perked it open again, ran down the path to the gate and mounted her horse Robin. MacHardie squinted keen old eyes and gave a grunt of amazement as the two rode off. If he could have believed his eyes, he was standing there by his own gate, watching himself ride off with his daughter Jean. He gave a dour grin, started for the house and turned to look again. Jean and her father, riding away up the trail to the Roberts ranch. The sharpest eyes in the country could think nothing else.

For more than half the distance no other eyes looked upon the two. But when they neared the gate cut into Dade's lower line fence for the convenience of those who rode that way, two horsemen appeared over a ridge toward the Tepee ranch and came on slowly, because of the packed and drifted snow, knee deep to their horses. They were making for the gate and the trail up the creek, no doubt about that. Than turned from a long stare and met Jean's startled eyes.

"We'd better hurry, sweetheart. You stop at the house and I'll go on, clear through and out the west gate, if necessary. If they take a notion to follow me, I'll keep going, that's all. Tell your dad I'll circle around back with his horse, sometime tonight. And you can say—"

"I'll say nothing of the kind. Pull up the muffler over your nose, as Father does sometimes, and let them come. But for your face, lad, I'd think myself ye were Father. Ye can nod and ye can shake yer head, mon, and if ye must speak, ye can growl and mumble and I'll tell them ye have a cold."

Than pulled up and swung stiffly down from the saddle. He slipped a gloved hand down the leg of MacHardie's horse, lifted the foot and laid it across his knee. "'Tis an onreasonable trail tae be pickin' up a wee bit rock in his fate," he remarked with an atrocious accent, "but 'tis a braw thocht tae gie' them the lead of us an' see whaur they're gaein' the noo."

207

Jean shook with laughter, not far short of being hysterical. "Than, quit it! You'll have Jock stampeding for home, if you keep that up. Dumb ye shall be, lad, if they speak to ye."

"Well, darn it, they'll beat us to the gate, anyhow."

"One of them is Blaney, lad."

"Good. I've got to see him. Who's with him? Dilly?" With his back to the riders, Than made a show of working over the sound foot of his mount.

She shaded her eyes against the sun glare on the snow. "Lad, 'tis Mr. Bearnson himself, I'm thinking." Her voice shook.

"I better turn back, then. You can get word to Blaney and have him come down. I've got to see him and tell him we've been framed on those worked brands. They'll think something's the matter with the horse."

"They will not. They're riding this way."

Than straightened, mounted. "All right then, let them come. I'll tell Bearnson to his face I'm onto his scheme. Come on, Jean."

To come sneaking back to his sweetheart like the thief he was not had been bitter enough. To be caught hiding within the clothes of her father was a worse humiliation, it seemed to him. He spurred forward, anxious to have it over with.

"Than! Than, are ye crazy?"

"Crazy to try and dodge," Than told her while he rode.

The two at the gate waited, Blaney off his horse and holding the gate open for these others to pass. His face was red with cold, grinning cheerfully as they came up.

"Hello, Jean. Howdy, Mr. MacHardie? Glad to see you folks. Saves me the ride down there. Heard the news, Jean? About the boys, I mean."

208

"And how should we hear news, then? Till now, I've not stirred from home since the storm, and neither has Father. Ye must excuse Father, Mr. Bearnson. Father has a verra bad cold and is that hoarse! Ye've no bad news, have ye, Blaney? Mr. Bearnson knows well 'twould be sore bad news for Father and me if the boys were caught."

Angus MacHardie was no more silent a man than Bearnson. He looked at Jean, cast a sharp glance at Than and grunted.

"They've got to be found, Jean. The sooner the better. That's why we're here—to tell all you folks the news." He looked at Bearnson. "Think it's premature, Mr. Bearnson, if I tell them?"

"Tell him," said Bearnson. "He'll run off again if you don't."

CHAPTER TWENTY-SIX

BLANEY STOOD BESIDE THE STOVE, HIS HANDS CLASPED behind him, fingers wriggling in the genial warmth. He looked at Than, sitting there frankly holding hands with Jean; at Susan, gazing up at himself as if he were a god; at Bearnson, straight-backed in his chair, with his hands on his knees; at Mom over across from him, with her skirts tucked close against her chair, as if she feared even they would be sullied by closer contact with her enemy.

"It gave me the creeps," Blaney went on, "just to hear the man boasting of the thing he had done. He had only one regret that I could discover, and that was that the cattle he had rebranded would go back to Mr. Bearnson. He was quite put out at that quirk of the law. He had

209

apparently gone ahead on the assumption that Bearnson would lose the stock. He said if he had stopped to think about the law restoring stolen property to its rightful owner, he would certainly have gotten busy and burned another corral or two of hay!"

Jean stirred, drew a deep breath. "Then it was Frank I saw ride into the gully before the fire."

"I suppose so. It must have been. He started the fire all right; he said so. He said he really didn't expect to burn quite so much territory, but he was glad Dade's buildings escaped. He seems to like Dade."

"And he didn't deny it when he sobered up?" Than asked. "He had an out there, if the fool had only known it. He could have claimed he was just talking to string you boys along."

"He tried that," Blaney said dryly. "It didn't work." He cast a sidelong glance at Bearnson.

Bearnson cleared his throat. "My men threatened to string him up to a beam in my big barn," he informed them, in his clipped colorless voice. "He begged me then to take him to Chinook, where the sheriff would protect him. I did so. He confessed to the District Attorney and was to plead guilty today."

"I sh'd think," Mom said tartly, "you'd of wanted to be right there and make very sure that Frank Hoskins was punished in the way he deserved. I would, if I'd known what was goin' on."

Somehow the room suddenly became very still. Eyes watched those two. It was coming; it was bound to come. The final duel of words, the widening breach or the practically impossible reconciliation between those two. Bearnson was inside Mom's house and he had not been scalded. His presence was tolerated. In the excitement, Mom had yielded so far, but her manner and her tone were hostile.

"I have a very good lawyer," Bearnson retorted. "One who does as he is told."

"Well," Mom said, with a click of her teeth, "it certainly is a surprise to me that you'd turn Frank Hoskins over to your lawyer and come off home without knowing what they'd done with him. When it was my two boys you were after, I notice you made it a point to get here yourself with the sheriff, just as quick as horseflesh could bring you! You didn't turn *that* case over to your lawyer, I notice!"

Bearnson gave her a cold stare. "You have yourself to blame for that, Mrs. Roberts. I admit there was a mutual misunderstanding about the fires. We both believed we had a grievance. But it was not Frank Hoskins who came to my place and deliberately attacked me. That you must admit was wholly uncalled for."

Mom's eyes sparkled behind her glasses. "Well, to my way of thinking, you never got a lick amiss, Pete Bearnson. If you didn't deserve it over our losing about everything in the world, you had it coming from away back in Helena."

"I never was in Helena."

Mom gave a ladylike sniff. "You needn't try to crawl out that way. You're old Pete Bearnson that used to run a store there. And a meaner old skinflint never walked."

Bearnson's face, red from the ten-mile ride in the cold, turned a darker shade. A vein on the side of his neck began beating quickly.

"I am not Pete Bearnson," he said, in the repressed tone of anger which is trying to be polite. "My name is Samuel Paul Bearnson and I have always been called Sam. I have a second cousin named Peter, who used to own a store somewhere in the southern part of the State.

I don't know him. Never saw him but once, when I was a boy in short pants. I certainly do not make myself responsible for his business methods. If you have any fault to find with mine, that is a different matter."

Mom gasped. "Well, for pity sake, why didn't you say so in the first place?"

"I was not aware that I was ever asked." Bearnson stood up, looked at Blaney.

Blaney shook his head. "I'll stay here, Mr. Bearnson. I want to make the trip back with Than to get his brother. And we haven't any too much time—" his glance strayed to Susan "—because there's a double wedding coming off, Christmas day. That's only a little more than a week from now. We'll have to hustle."

Bearnson—who was not Pete but Sam—took two steps and put out his hand to Than. "Sorry all this came up. Guess you've been made to suffer more than I have. I hope there's no hard feelings, young man."

"Not if you haven't, Mr. Bearnson." Than's look said that he meant it.

"I'm not a very good neighbor. Too busy with my own affairs. But I hope I'm not a bad one." He hesitated. "About this land: King, here, knew I had it under fence until such time as some one filed on it. I hope you didn't think I was capable of using underhand methods to drive you out. As a matter of fact, I was sorry to see the land taken. But since it was, I was glad to have respectable, quiet—er—people move in."

"Thinking what I thought about you, Sam Bearnson, you deserved every lick I give you!" Mom stoutly defended herself.

"Oh, go ahead and eat crow, why don't you, Mom?" Than urged her, grinning affectionately across at her. "It'll do you good."

212

"Jonathan, don't interrupt when older folks are talking. I was goin' to say, Sam Bearnson, that if you're a mind to let bygones be bygones, I'd like to have you stay to dinner. I've got baked beans in the oven and the brown bread's been steamin' itself to death. It won't take but a minute to make the coffee and set the table, and these boys 'll be wanting to get right back over there where David is. Thannie says David's got a good place to stay and plenty to eat, but it must be awful lonesome down in there all by himself and I want him brought home jest as quick as horses can travel."

Bearnson unbuttoned his overcoat again and let Susan take it and hang it behind the door. It didn't come down again until Than and Blaney were ready to start back after Dade, taking a packhorse this time and following the shorter route through Camas.

One thing more. On Christmas morning, six cows with their calves were found shut inside Than's corral. They had been Pothooks. Now they were Cross N's. But whether they were sent by Santa Claus to the family or were intended as a wedding present for Than, no one seemed to know. Both, probably. That is the way Than finally decided.

Oh, yes. Sam Bearnson and most of his cowboys attended the wedding. Bearnson brought the bill of sale, duly executed to Susan Elizabeth, Jonathan and David Roberts, and Blaney King. Which was explicit enough, surely.

We hope that you enjoyed reading this
Sagebrush Large Print Western.
If you would like to read more Sagebrush titles,
ask your librarian or contact the Publishers:

United States and Canada

Thomas T. Beeler, *Publisher*
Post Office Box 659
Hampton Falls, New Hampshire 03844-0659
(800) 818-7574

United Kingdom, Eire, and
the Republic of South Africa

Isis Publishing Ltd
7 Centremead
Osney Mead
Oxford OX2 0ES England
(01865) 250333

Australia and New Zealand

Bolinda Publishing Pty. Ltd.
17 Mohr Street
Tullamarine, 3043, Victoria, Australia
(016103) 9338 0666